YOUNG MARK

THE STORY OF A VENTURE

E. M. Almedingen

Young Mark

THE STORY OF A VENTURE

Illustrated by Victor G. Ambrus

FARRAR, STRAUS & GIROUX NEW YORK

An Ariel Book

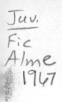

To F. M. PILKINGTON

Who—like Mark—would not be defeated by mere circumstance

Biographical Note

Mark Poltoratzky was born in Ukraina between 1726 and 1729, and died in St. Petersburg in 1789. He had one daughter and eight sons, one of whom was my great-grandfather. At Mark's death ten enormous estates were parceled out among his children.

He became something of a legend even in his lifetime. The reign of the Empress Elizabeth (1741–61) was marked by many examples of well-merited recognition given to talented nobodies. Mark's case was one in point. He was truly a nobody. His father may have enjoyed a great repute in Ukraina because of his horses, but Fedor Poltoratzky's grandiose stories about his exalted ancestry were so many fables. The name is not mentioned in any records, and it was certainly unknown in Russia until the middle of the eighteenth century. It was Mark's wonderful voice that raised the family to a pinnacle. He married a Princess Dolgoruka, and six of his eight sons chose their brides from the old aristocracy. His only daughter, Elizabeth, followed her own bent, and married a scholar and statesman of no high descent but of rare accomplishments, Alexis Olenin, at one time First Secretary of State and later Director of the Imperial Library in St. Petersburg.

It is possible that some direct descendants of Mark may still be living in England. Alexander Poltoratzky, his fourth son, came here in the retinue of the Emperor Alexander I in 1814 and married "the exceedingly beautiful Miss Dalrymple." He never went back to Russia, and his only daughter, Maria, married one Mr. Venables, a clergyman in Pembrokeshire.

In the family, stories of Mark's incredible rise to fortune were handed down from one generation to another. Inevitably, legendary touches crept into the narrative until it became rather difficult to tell truth from fiction. To me, it has always seemed odd that two of Mark's sons—Peter, who was a minor *lettré* in his generation, and Constantine, a soldier, who left most interesting memoirs of his share in the Napoleonic wars—had never attempted to tell their father's story, which, if handled by either of them, might have been clear of all legendary element.

At the end of the last century, some excerpts from Constantine's memoirs were published in one of the foremost historical reviews, and it was mentioned that the entire manuscript was in the Emperor's private archives and therefore beyond the reach of the public.

One of Mark's great-granddaughters, Hermione Poltoratzky, made a modest name for herself in the field of Russian historical studies. Some time between 1908 and 1913 Grand Duke Nikoli Mikhailovich, the historian, told her that during his researches in the Emperor's private archives (a member of the dynasty was allowed privileges denied to commoners), he came upon the manuscript of Constantine's memoirs. Scattered among those notebooks were several sheets and scraps of paper closely covered in a different handwriting. The Grand Duke had a look at some of them and found that they were reminiscences of Mark written by himself. My aunt Hermione could have no access to the emperial archives, and it must have been by the Grand Duke's courtesy that a transcript of those papers came into her hands. Then she discovered that they contained not—as she had hoped—the story of Mark's whole life but only a very detailed and somewhat confused recital of his adventures on the way to St. Petersburg. Evidently, those were the memories graven deepest in Mark's mind. Hermione Poltoratzky was disappointed but, the transcript having been lent to her, she duly copied it into her own notebooks—possibly in the hope of collecting enough material for a full biographical study. She died in 1916, that book still unwritten.

Many years ago those notebooks of hers came into my possession, and in my turn I laid them aside. Even a superficial study was enough to show that my great-great-grandfather was no accomplished man of letters. He remembered much and vividly, but he knew nothing of construction and his narrative sadly lacked in consecutiveness. It was impossible to trace his journey without the help of maps. In his pages, Romny preceded Mirgorod and Tver came before Moscow—on a journey northward! Quite a number of place names defeated all efforts at identification. Nor was he any more helpful in his dates. He remembered the years by seasons and Church festivals—he had no other calendar. Nonetheless, clumsy style and all the rest of it, Mark was a born writer—

the people he met on his arduous pilgrimage were real people and not wax dolls, and a birch coppice would suddenly come to life because he had slept there.

Except for the postscript—which is here rendered almost word for word—the book is no translation but rather as faithful a reconstruction as I could make of a venture at once splendid and foolhardy.

A glossary will be found at the end, together with a few explanatory notes—chiefly about such of the national customs as may not be intelligible to a Western reader.

E. M. Almedingen

Brookleaze
Bath, Somerset
August 1966

Contents

CONTENTS

YOUNG MARK

THE STORY OF A VENTURE

Explanatory notes begin on page 171 and a glossary on page 175.

1

The Way Toward a Decision

Let me but think of a cherry tree and a silver birch, and a whole world comes back to me. I can still see my father's *tabun* of some hundred-odd thoroughbred horses grazing in those immense fields edged by willows and oaks along the steep bank of the Dnieper. What a world it was—always exciting and wonderful, often dangerous and even frightening in spite of all the laughter, fun, and dancing which filled our leisure. You could not escape danger in a country like Ukraina, three ancient enemies for her close neighbors. Why, I can still hear my father's voice booming: "Try to run away from danger, and it will overtake you and break you bone from bone—as likely as not. Face it like a fighter, and it will make a man of you."

There was not much of a fighter in me. Nonetheless, I ran toward danger. I cannot tell if it made a man of me.

Our enormous steading, or *khutor,* lay on the western bank of the Dnieper. The sprawling whitewashed house looked like a toy in the immensity of field, meadow, and wood. It was a colorful toy. The slim, fluted pillars of the porch were painted blue and red. The tiny, crazily shaped windows were framed in green and yellow. The rooms were small and plainly furnished, but they, too, carried color. As to bodily comforts, few Ukrainian landowners thought of them at the time I was a boy. There was just one chair in the house—for my father's use. For the rest, there were trestles, chests, and tables rather artlessly made by home labor out of home-grown oak. The floors were of hard-beaten clay, they shone like silver, and a small rug was spread in the icon corner in every room.

Doors and windows were small and the walls were stout enough, but nothing could prevent the outer world from walking right into the house and filling it with several fragrances—mint and other herbs, sunflower seeds, apples, pears, mushrooms, and so often the cloying breath of watermelons' raspberry-colored flesh. There was also the smell of burning wax since few were the days when my mother did not light a candle in front of every icon.

I cannot remember much about the *gornitza,* a room kept painfully tidy for "company." My brothers and I were not encouraged to sit there. But the rest of the house was wholly ours. Straight from the porch you entered the common room, its roughly timbered walls hung all over with sabers, swords, muskets, daggers, and fishing rods. Beyond lay a spacious kitchen where my mother, Gapka the housekeeper, and other women did the cooking and where we all ate together—from my father down to the youngest poultry-yard girl. In a corner of the kitchen a crazily slanted ladder led to the loft, where fruit was kept and where my brothers and I slept on straw pallets. Our parents had a big wooden bed in the common room. Somewhere off the kitchen were little closets for Gapka, the maids, and my little sister, Fenia. Beyond, lay the dairy, larders, and stillroom.

4

The steading was immense. Not so the house, but to me it stood for a palace. Its name was "Bielogorka," Little White Hill, because of the silver birches. Our village, Malinovy Zviet, i.e. Raspberry Blossom, lay within an hour's ride from the manor. Two small fordable rivers ran in between. To Malinovy we rode on all the great feasts of the year—but hardly ever on ordinary Sundays. There was also the annual fair and about eight market days during the year. Not one of those would be missed. The country between the *khutor* and the village was my whole world through my childhood, a kindly and lovely world of orchard, meadow, wood, and large reaches of heath.

Now many people beyond the Ukrainian borders imagine that *khokhli,* i.e., the Ukrainians, are either peasants or Cossacks, with a thin sprinkling of magnates in their castles along the Polish frontier. But my father, Fedor Poltoratzky, was neither magnate nor peasant. Nor was he a Cossack, though in his day he had fought by their side against Pole, Turk, and Crimean Tartar. He was a landowner.

He was immensely proud of his name, and he would tell us that Bielogorka had been in our hands long before any tsar sat in Moscow. I could never understand how he knew it. There were neither books nor any documents in the house and, anyhow, my father was illiterate. But he never tired of telling us exciting stories about men and women of the family. One of them had married a king of Hungary. Another had gone to wed a "northern king." Hungary may have been on the moon for all we knew. We listened in silence because it was safer not to comment on my father's stories.

His Polish was halting and he never seemed at ease in Russian, though, by the time I was born, Ukraina had been under Russian rule for more than seventy years. Yet, whatever various treaties may have laid down, that lovely country still belonged to itself, and my father and all his friends looked upon the Russians as foreigners, and called them *Moskali,* contempt in their voices. They were all immensely tall, broad-shouldered men with incredibly long mustaches. They wore gray astrakhan caps even at the height of summer, and their wide dark-blue *sharovary* were tucked into shining knee-high boots. Horses and land was all they cared about, and my father's *tabun* was famous far beyond the neighborhood. A horse bred and broken in by Fedor Poltoratzky was a horse indeed and not just a four-footed animal. Later, I would learn that royal palaces in Sweden, Denmark, Poland, and Germany were glad to find stabling room for them.

My mother came of peasant stock from a village north of Poltava. She was as sturdy as a well-rooted apple tree, wise about the household, and rather reserved. Fenia alone was ever caressed by her, and that seldom enough. It was for my father to bring up his sons in as hard a way as he had been reared himself. Our infancy ended early enough, and one of the first lessons to learn was endurance. Neither a blizzard nor a deafening summer storm, neither frost nor heat were allowed to meddle with the day's jobs. Peasants from Malinovy kissed our parents' hands, bowed low from the hips, and called them "sir" and "madam," but we, their sons, grew up in the same way as a peasant's children except that we had more to eat and wore slightly better clothes on a feast day. Every square yard of my father's steading demanded work. The men in his service trained us, and they were told not to spare cuffs and kicks. Bean and turnip fields, meadows, woods, fields, orchards, outbuildings, and kitchen gardens—we learned the hard discipline of them all in the hardest possible way. The word "weariness" just did not belong to the household vocabulary—no matter how spent we were.

The care for the horses came first. Horses gladdened my father's heart and all but broke it.

There should have been ten of us, but four sons and two daughters had died in infancy. Mikhail, eleven years older than I, was the eldest. Then came Stepan, born in 1722, and I—four years later. Fenia, my sister, was just two years younger than I.

My father's first great grief was caused by Mikhail. 1734 was a terrible year. First a strange sickness fell on the *tabun,* many mares dying of it before they had foaled. Blight struck at barley and oats, and fodder had to be bought at a high price. On St. Peter's day, old Father Foma called in the afternoon. Mikhail, on seeing him come through the gate, ran up to the loft.

The priest came to tell my parents that Mikhail must be sent to the famous Theological Academy at Kiev. He had a vocation for the priesthood, said Father Foma.

My mother did not open the *gornitza* for the parish priest, and they were all in the common room. Running back to the house from the orchard, I halted, but nobody ordered me away and I sat on the bottom step of the porch. I was not big enough to understand all that was being said, but when I turned, I saw my father's frown and my mother's tears rolling down her seamed cheeks. Later my father explained to me that nobody could meddle with a vocation, but it was bitter for him to realize that his first-born would never rule at Bielogorka.

Now looking at my mother, I, too, felt near to tears. Then Mikhail came down from the loft, and he looked so pale that I thought he had been sick. I remember it all clearly because for the first and only time I saw my mother clasp Mikhail to her breast and kiss his forehead and cheeks, and I felt envious: she had never kissed either Stepan or me.

So Mikhail left Bielogorka, and not until two years had passed did he come back—for a short holiday—in a cleric's clothes, which looked odd on him. When he unpacked his bast hamper, I saw the very first books in my life, but they did not excite me much. Mikhail had become a stranger, and even his speech was hard for me to follow.

But I am running ahead.

That same summer of 1734 my father decided it was more than time for me to learn proper horsemanship.

Stable-work was among our daily duties, but the men did not like me in the stables. They complained that I could not keep quiet and that my clumsiness worried the horses. To my great relief, my father gave in to the men, and no summons to the stable yard now came to me. Nobody knew it, but I was terrified of horses. The mere sight of a stallion, however distant, filled me with horror all the deeper because I could not share my secret with anyone. Of course, I had ridden since before I could remember, as horses were our only means of transport except for ramshackle farm carts. But I had always ridden held in the crook of my father's strong arm, and I would feel safe.

Even now I shudder as I remember that summer morning.
My father had decided on Strawberry, a young, good-tempered roan mare. I had never been afraid of her and had
given her many a carrot, but that morning nobody thought of
carrots. My father, myself, Ilya—an outrider who would
follow me—and some three or four men made for the great
meadow which ran right down to the riverbank. I heard
someone whistle, and there was Strawberry quite close to me.
I stammered that I was sorry not to have brought a carrot, and
nobody answered. Within an instant Ilya picked me up and
had me mounted bareback—as was the fashion among us in
those days. Strawberry gave a whinny and was off.

I dug my hands into her mane and howled.

Later they would all say that it was my screaming that had
set her flying off. I could not tell. I screamed louder and louder,
and then loosed my hold and slipped off. I lay on the hot,
fragrant grass and heard hoofs somewhere behind me. I had
forgotten all about Ilya and imagined it was one of those
stallions galloping to trample me down. I closed my eyes tight.

The next thing I remember was sitting outside the back
door of the house and Gapka wiping my face with a cold wet
towel.

"I fell off," I stammered unnecessarily, and she pursed her
lips.

"I could not help it," I gulped, and she said roughly: "You
had no business to do it, more shame to you."

I did not see either of my parents again that day. Someone
brought me food, and I ate, leaning against the water butt in
the yard. It was a good dinner—cold cucumber soup and a

9

chunk of bacon—but I did not enjoy it. I knew I was in disgrace.

Later, up in the loft, I said to Stepan: "I could not help slipping off."

Stepan scowled. "You should be wearing Fenia's petticoats."

With but four years between us, Stepan and I should have been comrades. He would not have it so, however, and he remained a padlocked room to me to the very end.

Next morning I saw my father in the back yard. My heart all but thudded, but he spoke kindly: "Well, Mark lad, you will never make much of a horseman, will you?"

I hung my head for shame.

"Strawberry is all right," he went on. "Ilya caught up with her just in time."

I raised my head a little.

10

"Now off with you to the turnip field, lad." He turned away, and I ran, my thoughts all in a tangle. I had expected the worst beating in my life.

Soon after, Bobyla, my godfather, rode over to Bielogorka. The meal was laid in the *gornitza,* my sister being banished into the kitchen. Stepan and I, each given a huge cabbage pasty, were ordered to make ourselves scarce, so that I guessed Bobyla had been invited for a serious discussion. Stepan at once made for the stables. I ate my pie, straddling across a limb of an old lime close to the house. Nobody could see me there, nor could I see much, but the windows stayed open. I meant to hear all that would be said.

Bobyla towered even over my father. He had silver platters in his house, large turquoises studded his bridle, and summer and winter alike he swathed his enormous neck in a piece of garnet-colored velvet. He was good-natured, brave, and generous. His appetitie had been legendary since his youth. He could dispatch a roast goose and fifteen fried eggs at a sitting. Little wonder that my mother and the women had been hustling about in the kitchen since daybreak.

Ah, that meal! I got a cramp first in my right leg, then in my left, and still they went on eating, all the good smells nearly maddening me. As they ate, they talked of horses, crops, the Crimean khan, the king of Poland, and various troubles along the western border. Was it for that, I asked myself, that we children had been banished from the house? Suddenly I heard my father thump his fist on the table and plunge into the pitiful story about Strawberry and me.

"And what do I do now?" he thundered. "Mikhail is gone and Stepan's set his mind on joining the Tsarina's army."

I heard and nearly fell off the tree. Fancy Stepan having enough pluck to set his mind on anything!

"Well," boomed Bobyla, "nobody could turn a goose into a heron, Fedor. Have that daughter of yours married to a good lad, and he will carry on here. Talked to Father Foma, have you?"

"Why should I?" my father broke in impatiently. "That is not a priest's business."

"But Mark is a stout lad for all that," ruminated Bobyla. "I mind well him falling off that apple tree. Gashed his thigh, he did, and never a whimper."

"I'd have leathered him hard if he had," retorted my father.

"Leave the lad be, Fedor," said Bobyla. "Time will show."

"Yes, so you say, but one of the men told me that Mark will shy off at the mere sight of a stallion. Fancy me having a son like that! What would Bielogorka be without my horses, I ask you."

"A wilderness, Fedor, a wilderness," said Bobyla comfortably. "Time will show. We'll talk about it again come Christmas. God reward you both for the good cheer and the welcome."

I made it my business to be near the porch at my god-father's departure. I hoped to get the usual copper coin from him, but I never got one that day. He saw me, fumbled in his enormous pouch, slipped something into my hand, and then slapped my back so hard that I all but measured my length on the sand.

Now, with my parents speeding Bobyla off, I, my thanks stammered, ran to the orchards. All by myself, I unclenched my hot palm. Bobyla had given me a gold piece, a real, heavily minted *chervonetz*.

I felt almost dizzy. I licked it and bit it. Then I made my way into the loft. There, just over my pallet, hung an icon of St. Mark's. It had a small opening at the back to house a relic, but at Bielogorka nobody bothered much about relics. I slipped my treasure inside and rehung the icon carefully. When my mother said that now I could spend "the copper piece" at the Assumption Fair outside Malinovy, I said I would.

One season followed another. Mikhail would come home for a bit, more and more of a stranger every time, his hair and hands smelling of wax and incense, and his speech laden with too much piety to please my father. Stepan went on in his way, and so did I, spending what little leisure I had on the riverbank, listening to the water and the birds.

I believe I was about eleven when something burst upon me. Stepan had set his heart on soldiering, and I—oh dear, how hard it was not to have a soul to share my discovery with. . . .

It happened in May. The weather was perfect, and all the orchards were drowned in color. My morning's stint done, I made my way to the river. The floor of the silver-birch wood was enameled with loosestrife, wild narcissus, cuckoo spit, harebells, and wild strawberries—pink on white, red on blue, white on yellow and orange—a carpet no mortal woman could have woven. I threw myself down under an old lime and stared at the Dnieper running far below. Suddenly, a blackbird alighted on a bough of a neighboring birch and sang, and I answered him.

I had been singing since my early childhood. Everybody

who had anything of a voice did—and still does—in my country. We sang at play and at work—mostly old folksongs, and singing with us was as natural as putting a shirt on in the morning. If Gapka did not sing when mixing the dough for *vatrushki*, the sweet cheese tarts which could be made by none but a Ukrainian woman, my mother might have wondered if the woman had a stomach ache or something.

But that May morning it was different. Somehow I knew that my voice meant far more than Bobyla's gold coin so jealously hidden in the loft, and I cannot tell how I knew it. I was quite ignorant. I could no more read music than make out the letters of the alphabet. But I did know that I had been given a treasure and that I was facing a tremendous challenge.

I kept it all to myself. A year passed and another, and there was much talk about fighting Turkey, and Stepan joined the Tsarina's army. I believe my mother wept in secret. My father's face was as dark as a thundercloud on an August day, and so it continued for many days.

And then it was Easter once again. Of all the feasts, I held it dearest because it answered everything I knew in my small world—new grass, first swelling buds, deep breaths of soil released from the yoke of snow and ice. That Easter my father gave me a splendid new belt, a broad one made of fine scarlet cloth and studded all over with tiny gilt buttons.

In the late afternoon of Easter Eve, we all rode to Malinovy for *zautrenia,* the midnight service. I went with Gapka and another woman in the creaking farm cart drawn by two oxen, with old Gridko on the box. The cart was loaded with traditional Easter fare presently to be blessed by the priest—hams studded with cloves, baskets of red-painted eggs, big cream cheeses, and several Easter cakes called *babi*. There was a big hamper of other good things, my father's Easter offering to the priest.

The cart jogged on slowly from one rut to another. Gridko was too deaf to talk to. The two women fell into a doze. The soft westerly wind carried the smell of wet grass and soil. I sniffed hungrily. Then I listened. The wind seemed to sing about the spring.

I was looking forward to the great annual service. One particular anthem said much to me—"Be thou holy, be thou holy, New Jerusalem, because the glory of the Lord shines upon thee." I loved the word "glory"—in Old Slavonic, *Slava*. It sounded such a triumphant word, and I remembered a lark I had not seen but heard that very morning.

"He had his share of Easter," I thought.

Slava—a glorious word indeed, but at Malinovy there was nobody to share such splendors with. The old, sour-tempered deacon would have thought me mad, and the clerk was no better. Between them, they could not manage the choir, raw village lads all of them, whose one idea of rendering glory to the Lord was to shout at the top of their bent. It was really curious—how well they all sang in the fields or on the river— but once within that ugly timbered church their voices became so many tautened wires.

We reached Malinovy, and I helped the women to arrange the food along trestles outside the crazily slanted porch of the little church. Then I followed my parents inside. The service began. It was a long time before that particular anthem was due to be sung, and I cannot now remember what my thoughts were about. At the right moment, before the deacon or the choir could realize what was happening, I opened my mouth. Nobody interrupted me. I reached the last words hardly aware of what I had done. Then I got the hardest kick ever from my father, together with the curt order to be off. Flushed, a little shaken, but intensely happy, I threaded my way through the crowd to the door.

In the end, it was not a particularly cheerful Easter at Bielogorka. Men and women of the household kept shaking

their heads and muttering among themselves. Few of them exchanged the traditional triple kiss with me. My mother looked as though the Day of Judgment were around the corner, and my father ignored me altogether. Everybody made it obvious that my performance during the Easter service had disgraced the name of Poltoratzky, and I am ashamed to say that I did not care in the least.

A few days later, the old priest called at Bielogorka. On seeing his shabby cart at the gate, I took instant refuge in the old lime tree. He went into the common room and refreshments were offered to him. I heard him wheezing refusal and acceptance almost in the same breath.

Then he said:"With such a voice, the lad might end as an archdeacon. You should send him to be trained at Kiev."

"No," thundered my father. "It is bad enough to have one son trailing about in a cassock. And you sould be ashamed of yourself, Father. You should have sent the deacon or someone to stop the boy."

"You are out of your wits." The old priest raised his voice. "Stop him? I could have listened to him forever. Talk of a nightingale . . . I tell you even a cathedral chapter in St. Petersburg would be proud to have him. What is more, Fedor, there is talk about Princess Elizabeth becoming Empress, and she is partial to our countrymen because of Alexis Razumovsky.* People say she means to have the Hetman for her husband."

"I don't care a sunflower seed about your cathedrals," my father broke in, but Father Foma went on as though there had been no interruption: "Of course, the lad must be properly

* See note on page 172.

18

trained. Yes, he must go to Kiev, Fedor. There is much nonsense in him, but they will beat it all out of him. It is a sin to go against God's will, Fedor."

The argument went on for some time. At last my father said wearily, "I suppose you would know more about God's will than anyone else. Well, then, when do I send the lad?"

"In the autumn, and I can arrange—" replied Father Foma, and my father broke in haughtily: "There is no need to. I have kinsmen in Kiev."

I climbed down the lime tree and wandered off to the orchard. I clearly knew what I was going to do, but my plan had nothing to do with any Theological Academy in Kiev or anywhere else.

2

That Long, Long Waiting

I made up my mind that I would be a singer, and that to me did not mean Kiev but much, much farther away. I meant to get to St. Petersburg—all on my own. Beyond that, I knew nothing at all. I indulged in no dreams. I built no plans. I knew I had to wait, and the waiting proved long and hard. But the decision once made, I knew I could do no other. I had never traveled beyond Malinovy and I had a vague idea that St. Petersburg was somewhere at the end of the world. Sometimes that frightened me. Again it spurred me on. But it was hard to have no one to share the secret with me.

My resolve not to be sent to Kiev gained strength every time Mikhail came home from his Academy. He had become a whey-faced stranger who looked upon the land with jaundiced eyes. He would help with the hay harvest so reluctantly that my father all but lost his temper.

"Take off that cassock of yours and work like a man, will you?"

Mikhail would purse his lips, snatch at the hone, and start sharpening his scythe.

"That is not the way to hold it," shouted my father. "Do

you think a scythe is a woman's needle? Did I not flog you enough?"

Mikhail never answered. The work done, he would vanish up into the loft and bury himself in his books, which smelled of wax and incense. I felt at once sorry and contemptuous. Mikhail had been brought up in as hardy a way as Stepan and I, but it looked as though the Theological Academy had turned him into a lump of cream cheese.

Three things happened during that dreadful summer. First, I had my fourteenth birthday and not even Gapka remembered it. Indeed, how could anyone remember anything as insignificant after the supper the evening before? We had finished eating, the serving folk had gone, but we lingered in the kitchen, the door open. It was a lovely silver June night, and I longed to run down to the riverbank, but none of us dared get up from the table until my father gave us leave. He sat there, drumming on the table and staring at Mikhail.

"You'll be priested come Easter," he said gruffly. "I must send word to that widowed sister of Bobyla's. Her youngest, Nastia, would do for you. Not much of a dowry there, but that does not matter."

I pricked my ears. I did not then know that in our Church men had to get married before ordination. If their wives died, they could not marry again. I had not met Bobyla's niece. I wondered if Mikhail had—not that it mattered. In those days it was for the parents to choose brides and grooms for their children. I saw my mother smile as she peered into a half-empty *zhban* of raspberry water and I saw Mikhail flush.

"Nastia can leave her home for Kiev—she has an uncle there," my father went on. "She can be married from there. We have no time for all that fuss at Bielogorka. Your mother has plenty of household gear to spare, and we'll send it up by water."

Mikhail seized a blue-painted wooden spoon and clutched it so hard that his knuckles went white.

"Lost your tongue, have you?" inquired my father.

My brother raised his head and let go the spoon.

"I—I—am not going to marry—anyone—"

"Not going to—" My father clenched his fists.

"I—I—am going to—to—to Pechera Abbey—" stuttered Mikhail.

22

My mother crossed herself. My father stared, breathing heavily. Then he roared: "Want to become a *chernetz,* do you? Bad enough to have a priest for a son, but a monk—"

Mikhail said nothing. My mother stood up, and for the first time I learned how brave she could be.

"God forgive you for such words, Fedor. If the boy wishes to go to Pechera, let him. His prayers might help us to get rid of our sins—"

"Silence," thundered my father, but it was she who silenced him. She never raised her voice, and I can't now remember all she said, but in the end my father stumped out of the kitchen, and that night he slept outside, under the great elms in the yard.

He never spoke to Mikhail again, nor do I remember any further visits of Father Foma. Soon afterward he died, and a younger man came to Malinovy. My father went on paying the customary parish dues, but the newcomer remained a stranger.

A few days after Mikhail's departure for Kiev, I met my father in the orchard.

"Lad," he said gruffly, without looking at me, "I am not going to ask the parish clerk to write to our folk at Kiev. You would be wasted there."

I pretended to be upset and began rubbing my eyes on the sleeve of my smock.

"Stop sniveling." He bent toward me and shook me hard. "How old are you? Thirteen? Fifteen?"

"Fourteen, Father."

"Well, I have got an eye on a good bridegroom for Fenia. Once they are betrothed, he'll be one of the family and look

23

after the *tabun*. And you are to stay here, see? You are middling good at field work and much else, and Nastia will be your wife. I mean to get the betrothal articles signed next Easter."

I heard. There seemed nothing to say, and I said nothing.

On St. Peter's day Nastia and her mother came over for the day. The plump, red-cheeked mother was all butter and honey. A widow, she was left with ten children, six daughters among them, and I suppose a bridegroom like myself was a good fish to her net.

But if the mother was all honey, Nastia seemed as sour as an overpickled cucumber. She spoke civilly enough to my parents, but she stared at me as though I were a bear cub, and I saw her pinch little Fenia's arm —all on the sly. Nastia wore so many strings of beads that you could not see the color of her bodice, her mouth was thin and she kept pursing it, her brown eyes changed their expression from one moment to another, and I thought to myself: "That is a girl who would pretend cabbage was pink if it suited her book."

Fenia was ordered off to the kitchen to help Gapka, and I

24

was told to take Nastia over the steading. At a corner of the stable yard a young puppy rushed toward us and began rolling at our feet. Nastia kicked him hard. He whimpered and scuttled away. The blood rushed into my face.

"What did you do that for?" I snapped at Nastia.

"He got into my way. I might have fallen and muddied my kirtle," she said calmly.

I knew I hated her. We had no further conversation. At the end of the day, when they were gone, my mother asked: "Well, Mark, how did you get on?"

I stammered awkwardly: "She is just a girl, isn't she?" and I added, "Her beads did jingle, didn't they?"

Fenia smothered a giggle. My mother frowned. My father helped himself to some more cold goose, and nothing else was said. It was a relief to climb up to my loft. A short prayer mumbled, I sprawled on my pallet, vowing that I would never marry my godfather's niece.

A little later came a feast day. We had company for dinner. My mother, Gapka, and the other women had been at it since dawn, and the kitchen was as steamy as the bathhouse on a winter's day. The weather being fine, we ate in the open. There was pumpkin soup, a huge joint of pickled beef, and a suckling pig roasted with herbs; there were mountains of *galushki* and *tvorog* with cream. My mother put out the best silver goblets and the spoons with carved ebony handles. As I sat on the grass, hearing the guests' laughter and talk and enjoying my share of the good things, I felt happy, and the scent of bruised grass at my feet meant Bielogorka and all it stood for—the beauty, the space, and the orderliness. It was a life which flowed in obedience to the demands of the four seasons. That day I loved it all dearly.

I had finished my share of the beef, and a serving woman had just filled my platter with steaming galushki, when the storm broke, though the skies overhead remained blue.

At first we all thought the man was a beggar, so dusty his clothes, so weary his face. But he proved no beggar; he was a soldier from the Tsarina's army, and he carried a crumpled piece of gray paper in his right hand. His face was lean and gray, and he looked like a man who brought no good news with him. Everybody stopped eating and laughing. Everybody stared. My father rose.

"Christ bring you to my board, stranger," he said politely, since such was our custom.

The man bowed awkwardly and stretched out his hand. The dirty gray paper fluttered in the breeze.

"No good your giving papers to me, stranger," said my father. "I have never been taught my letters—"

"I come from Poltava, sir," the man said in an oddly tautened voice. "I am a sergeant in the Tsarina's army, and I bring you sorrow, sir. Your son Stepan has been killed by the Crimean Tartars. It is all in the paper." He paused and added, "I saw him fall. He was a brave lad."

A loud wail interrupted the stranger. Her face covered by the gay Persian shawl, my mother staggered to her feet and made toward the house. Gapka and the other women followed her, all wailing. They must have gone to the very back of the house, because the sound of their crying grew thinner and thinner. In the great courtyard, all the guests kept silent, and my father got up, a goblet in his hand. His voice did not shake when he asked them to drink for the repose of the soul of his son Stepan, and they drank in silence. I stared at the pale golden *galushki* on my platter and then scrambled to my feet and stole away, none of them taking notice of me.

I knew I could not face the women in the kitchen. So the loft was out of the question. I made for the riverbank instead, threw myself under a thick-girthed lime, and thought. I felt no grief for Stepan—he had always been so distant; but for the first time I wondered whether we meant anything to my father apart from our being useful about the place. He had quarreled with Mikhail for going to the monastery. He had been furious with Stepan for joining the army, but the news brought by that soldier did not seem to have shaken him. Had Stepan lived, he would have stayed in the army for more than twenty years.

My thoughts may have been muddled, but I remember that my resolve to run away became much stronger that day. I just did not see why I, the only remaining son, should be cheated out of a possible chance, and a little later I dared greatly and braved my father's anger.

"Mikhail has done what he wanted. So did Stepan—"

"Well?" He stared at me.

"Can't I do what I want, too?"

"Well?" he said again as indifferently as though I were a fly buzzing over his head.

I gulped hard. "I want—to sing—"

"So it is Kiev you are hankering after?" he asked mockingly, and I clenched my fists.

"No, Father. They would turn me into a cleric there. I don't want to be either priest or monk." I added rather clumsily: "And I hope to get married, too—"

He thrust both hands into his belt.

"You are to be betrothed at Easter," he said levelly. "Sing? You can sing all day if it pleases you."

"I did not mean that . . . I want to learn notes and everything."

For a moment I thought my father would strike me, but he merely measured me with a glance.

"And I want you to clean out the pigsties." His voice was harsh. "Yes, this very morning. Be off with you."

That was the kind of job his hirelings would be set to, and my fury leaped to a peak as I ran toward the great yard.

The work took me a long time—inexperienced as I was— and when I had finished I knew that my love for Bielogorka had gone somewhere into a corner so dark I could not see it.

On Assumption Day there was a fair at Malinovy. I had some hours of leisure, but my father never gave me the usual copper. Gapka alone was marvelously kind and filled a satchel with good things to eat. I trudged to Malinovy on foot, and having wandered from one stall to another, heavily conscious of having not a single coin to spend, I left the fairground for a vast field outside. There, under a stunted oak, I saw a lad sprawling on the grass. His clothes excited me. Never before had I seen anyone wearing a green coat with scarlet breeches. Slim, bronzed of face, he seemed slightly older than I. He grinned and invited me to share his dinner— a couple of onions and a chunk of bread. His speech told me that he was no Ukrainian.

It seemed good to find a companion that day. I stretched myself on the hot stubble, untied the satchel, and shook out its contents. Gapka had indeed been generous: a leg of roast goose, three mushroom pasties, a huge *vatrushka*, a chunk of bacon, and four apples. The boy stared at the spread, whistled, and licked his lips.

"What a feast! Why, you must come from a manor."

"Don't you?" I asked politely.

He laughed and did not answer. I found my pocketknife and began cutting the bacon. He watched me, himself motionless, and I knew that I liked him. Anyone else would have grabbed at the food. He had to be persuaded to share it.

We ate in silence. Then I ventured: "Where do you come from?"

"I was born north of Moscow."

"Does your family—" I began, and he shook his head.

"I have no family. There is an aunt somewhere—but I don't know if she is alive. I travel about"—he paused and added proudly—"and I earn my living."

The scarlet breeches and the green coat looked stained and shabby. The provender he had was certainly meager, and I had never heard about a lad north of Moscow earning his living at Malinovy.

"I have come with the fair people," he explained.

"What do you do?"

"Oh, anything—sing, dance, crack jokes, mime—"

"Mime?" I caught at the unfamiliar word.

"Why, yes. Anything to amuse the good folk. We go from one fair to another. People like getting some fun at times. Life is not a buttered bun for many, is it?"

"But what is mime?" I insisted.

"Don't you know? Why, I'll show you," and he leaped to

his feet, slim, wiry, alive from the top of his tousled head to the toes of his broken boots, and I knew that I liked him more and more.

He pulled off his scarlet coat, and I saw a dirty tattered shirt; he drew in his shoulders, thrust his chin forward, and shook his hair all over his forehead. His eyes grew smaller and his mouth caved in as though he had not got a tooth in his head. I watched, fascinated, and his voice was the voice of a very old man, tremulous and pathetic. He had had his only coat stolen from him and winter was around the corner. I felt like weeping and laughing at the same time. When the lad suddenly swung around, picked up the coat, flung it over his shoulders, I laughed to tears.

"You are clever," I said. "That old man was there! And they pay you for it?"

"Of course. I could mime a vagrant monk begging, and a fisherman with a torn net, and all sorts of other things, too. I love doing it."

"It is a good life."

"And a hard one, little brother."

I said wistfully, "I'd like to join you."

"You—from a manor and all? You'll never stand it."

"I live hard," I protested. "I sleep on straw."

"That is nothing. In Moscow I once heard of a countess whose children slept on straw. No," he went on, "it is often hunger and cold, and days when you feel your feet don't belong to you, so tired they are. And we don't get much of a welcome anywhere, except at fairs and suchlike. People think we are thieves and vagabonds." He laughed. "Vagabonds we are indeed—all the time—and thieves, too, sometimes. Hunger drives you that way."

"What's your name?" I asked suddenly.

"Petka, and what is yours?"

I told him, and he stared at me very hard.

"Anyway, what could you do on the road—bred the way you must have been?"

"Sing." I spoke boldly, broke off a blade of grass, and began chewing it.

"Well, what about giving me a song, eh?"

I hesitated—but the vast field seemed deserted except for the two of us. Then I took a deep breath and sang a short piece about the reeds asleep on the Dnieper through a June night. I finished and glanced at Petka. Hands behind his back, he lay on the grass and gaped at me.

"Little brother," he stuttered, "what a voice! But you must not go wandering about fairs . . . Not the right thing at all."

I said nothing. I was resolved to keep my plan a secret from

everybody in the world, and it startled me to hear Petka say, "But you should get away from villages."

"Where to?"

"St. Petersburg."

I gasped and still I said nothing.

"Yes, that would be the making of you—all on your own, mind. You'll get there all right—brigands and bears and all—I am sure you will. There is good stuff in you." He went on, "You know we have a baby Tsar now?"

I shook my head.

"Surely we have a Tsarina?"

"Heavens, is Ukraina like the moon?" he laughed. "Tsarina Anna died a year ago. It is Ivan, her great-nephew, but folks say he won't last, see? It is all Germans now, and it is Princess Elizabeth they want for Tsarina, and she favors your people. There is a very grand *khokhol* she means to marry."

But such high matters were beyond my comprehension. Looking away from Petka, I asked carefully: "Why do you think I should get away?"

"To find your feet, lad," he replied very seriously. "I am just a vagabond and so are all my mates. We could be of no use to you, but I reckon it would be a sin to waste such a voice." He rose and clapped me on the shoulder. "God bless you for the bread and salt. Good luck to you!" He paused. "I should stay the winter through and make for the north around about Easter if I were you."

I made an effort and shook my head.

"Petka, I have never been beyond Malinovy."

"That is like an acorn saying it would never grow into an oak," he broke in, and ran off. I was never to meet him again.

My own plan still a jealously hoarded secret, I trudged home, my thoughts all on fire. Even Petka's words about brigands and bears could not scare me. His praise had certainly flattered me. His suggestion—so unaccountably at one with my own wishes—was like a beacon. I whistled and hummed as I walked back to Bielogorka.

At supper that evening Gapka asked what I had done with the satchel.

"It was the best one—with leather thongs," she said.

"I am afraid I have lost it," I muttered, and my father cuffed me soundly.

I got up to my loft, knelt by the little window, and talked to the night. I just had to share that wonderful day with someone.

3

The Waiting Ends

I can't now remember much about that winter except that it came early enough and everybody talked about an early spring. There were terrible blizzards, and Bielogorka was cut off from the outside world till well after Christmas. As usual, life in the house became a closed-in business. Even to cross the yard you had to smother yourself in sheepskins and put on knee-high felt boots. My mother and sister kept indoors most of the time. They were always occupied, and my mother did not like talking when she had the needle in her hand. I carved wooden spoons, soldered caldrons, cleaned my father's arms and harness, fetched water for the kitchen women, swept the snow at the back door, and, as usual, was at everybody's beck and call. My father spent much time in the stables. When he came indoors, he either ate or slept in his huge chair. He looked morose and I avoided him as much as I dared.

He slept much. Whenever he did, nobody dared sing at their work. It was a stifling silence to me.

We would sup early because my mother was rather careful with the candles. The meal over, I would be sent up to the loft, where I was not allowed even a tallow dip. Some warmth

would steal up the ladder from the kitchen. I would huddle
on my pallet, sheepskins for my blanket, think of my gold
piece, St. Petersburg, Petka, and a future I could not even
imagine clearly, and then fall asleep.

It was a hard winter within and without. I was still among
them and yet I felt an outsider. Gapka and old Gridko would
tease me about Nastia, and I got sick of the very sound of the
name. My little sister, her day's chores done, became something of a limpet. She, too, would whisper about Nastia,
whom she disliked for being a telltale. Fenia hated the idea of
Nastia's coming to Bielogorka, and it was often hard for me
not to turn around and blurt out, "You need not fret. She will
never come."

There was nothing amusing except one brief moment at
Christmas. There was no question of riding to Malinovy
because of the blizzards. We feasted at home in the traditional
way with bean soup and pickled ham for supper, the great gilt
star hung in the corner of the common room. We sang the old

song about the Magi and the Infant in the manger, but nobody felt really festive because of my father's ill humor. And suddenly, when the song was finished, Fenia burst out: "And did God's mother see it all happen?"

For no reason that I could see, the naïve question brought warmth into the room. Even my mother smiled and my father's frown vanished. Gapka and the others were giggling, aprons to their mouths.

"See it happen, little one?" boomed my father, and Fenia blushed.

"Well, I just wondered, because she was up in heaven, wasn't she?"

It was indeed a light moment, but it went and there came no others that I can remember. Bielogorka's life went on from day to day, and I said to myself that it would go on just the same once I had gone.

My resolve to leave gathered strength as the winter went on, but I was so ignorant. I had never been beyond Malinovy. I knew that somewhere, far up the river, was Kiev and all its marvels, which I did not wish to see. Somewhere far beyond the eastern bank of the Dnieper lay Poltava, and much farther on, Moscow, and then—virtually at the end of the world—St. Petersburg. I also knew that down to the south, where the Dnieper looped sharply to the west, were the terrible Zaporozhy Rapids. I knew no more than that, and I had never seen a map. On the other hand, the ways of all the seasons were familiar to me; so was the course of a wind and the map of the sky. I could tell the spoor of a boar and make out the track of a hare, and I knew how to keep clear of all boggy and marshy patches. My father's men approved my swimming, and I was passably good at managing a raft. I told myself that my one blind spot was my fear of unbroken horses.

I reckoned it would take me all of a summer to reach the Far North. In my neighborhood, people measured a distance by the time it took to get from one place to another—an hour's ride, four hours' tramp, and so on. I had my jealously hoarded gold piece, but I decided not to spend it and to earn shelter and victuals by singing.

My objective was the north, and Malinovy lay to the north of us, but I knew I must not be seen near the village. That meant crossing the river by Bielogorka, and the Dnieper was not fordable at that place.

There was a spot near the bank which I preferred to all others—a patch of tangled undergrowth, with a few gnarled old elms in the middle. Nobody ever went there and not even little Fenia knew of it. That corner became my headquarters as soon as the blizzards had stopped.

I had never made a raft in my life, but I had seen some being made, and I hoped I could do it. I meant it to be very small, and there was no difficulty in getting hold of a few well-planed pieces of seasoned oak. My father would often employ me on various carpentering jobs about the steading, and I knew where to look for a hatchet, nails, a long piece of stout rope, and a bucket of tar. I was like a cat in the dark and it was no effort to carry all the wood and the tools to the secret spot near the riverbank. The work took much longer than I had thought since it required much ingenuity to steal an hour or so of daylight. But when it was done, it looked a proper raft, which, however small, was no toy.

Easter fell so late that year that I could count on the

Dnieper being clear of ice, but when I had finished the raft, a worm of an idea crept into my mind and stayed there. I meant to run away and I had no regrets—but I must leave a message behind, and how could I do it when I did not know my letters? For me to vanish without a word would mean an immediate search all over the neighborhood, and I would most probably be found and brought back to Bielogorka, and I did not like to think about the consequences. But if my father had a message, he would send for the old parish clerk whom he trusted and have it read to him, and I knew him well enough to realize that his pride would insist on letting it rest there. "I should have asked Mikhail to teach me the alphabet," I thought.

There was just nobody in my little world to leave a verbal message with. The men liked me well enough, but not one of them would have risked my father's anger. Nor would Gapka or any other woman about the place.

So worried did I get that my mind began slipping away from the work I was doing. Once in the kitchen, I dropped a cooper kettle and dented it so badly that my mother boxed my ears, though Gapka grinned.

"Ah, but the lad is thinking of his betrothal day," she said.

Yet luck did not turn its back on me. It happened in this way.

It needed but ten days till Passion Sunday and we were all in the common room before dinner when my father stopped polishing an old saber, stamped his foot, and muttered: "Here all the men are hard at work, and I can't spare the time either, and there are my boots and the boy's waiting at Yanko's, and how could I get them from Malinovy, I ask you?"

My mother quietly folded the towel she was hemming.

"Can't the boots wait till after Easter?"

"What? Go to Easter Mass in my old boots?" thundered my father. "Wife, you've mislaid your wits."

"There is old Gridko."

"I might just as well send Cherry the cow—"

I heard it all and went on rubbing bear grease into my father's saddle. Suddenly I heard my mother say: "Well, husband, Mark could fetch the boots. He has been working hard lately—let him have a day off."

39

I felt like leaping in the air, but I kept still. My father stroked his mustaches.

"Well, why not?" he said at last. "So long as he is back by sundown. Do you hear, lad? You'll get a whipping if you are late."

Most fervently did I promise to be back by sundown. I had not had a day all to myself since before Christmas, and the prospect of a good long wander was better than a warm bed on a cold night.

The next morning broke mild and clear, softly flounced clouds riding across a pale blue sky. Breakfast over, I scrambled into my sheepskins and boots and was off.

The orchards left behind, I plunged into a wide ride across our beech wood. The snow had lost its firmness and color. It lay in uneven gray-yellow patches here and there, and I could almost hear the sap stir in every tree. As I went on, I saw that the March sun had worked its will on the snow—young grass was pushing up here and there, and what runnels I came across flashed clear of the very last splinter of ice. I unbuttoned my sheepskins and breathed hungrily. Hope lay upon the land and hope was in my heart. I even stopped fretting about that message I could not leave behind. I said to myself, "That'll take care of itself when the time comes," and I leaped for sheer joy, slipped on an icy patch, measured my length on the hard, cold soil, and laughed as I picked myself up.

Never had the familiar way to Malinovy seemed so short. I did not walk: I ran. I felt as though I were winged. I suppose I must have had a presentiment that the day would prove a landmark. I can't tell.

At last I reached the village, the ugly dull blue cupola of

the wooden church gleaming in the sun, the priest's humpy little house nestling close by. I saw the huddle of huts, their whitewashed walls certainly cleaner than the dirty trodden snow in the middle of the street. An ox stood ruminating in a tumbledown gateway, cattle were lowing and geese cackling, men shouting at their work in the back yards, and, as usual, a bunch of shawled women stood chattering by the well.

I shouted the customary greetings as I ran to Yanko's hut right at the very end of the street. Yanko, a small spare man with a raveled reddish beard and sharp green eyes which would have found a needle in a haystack at a glance, so folks said, was cobbler, farrier, and medicine man to the entire neighborhood. There were whispers that he also meddled in matter no Christian should have known anything about, but that never troubled me. I liked the man's talk and he usually had something exciting to say.

Yanko certainly did not disappoint me that day.

The beautiful new boots paid for and safely tucked away in my satchel, he grinned at me.

"There is a visitor." He gestured toward a sledge outside the priest's house. "If you had a message for Father Siemen, young sir, you would meet him. Yes, a visitor all the way from Poltava—braved the bad roads and all. A cousin to the priest he is and a clerk in some office. And his talk is like silk." Yanko grinned again and stroked his beard. "They say he has been prowling here, there, and everywhere—looking for a young lady he is—a count's daughter or a prince's, I can't rightly say. Ran away from home, she did, a while back. I reckon the gentleman got tired of searching and thought a day or two at Malinovy would not hurt anyone."

41

I listened hungrily. At once I remembered my mother wondering whether the priest and his wife—both more or less strangers to us—would like a tablecloth or a linen bedspread for an Easter gift, and I said loftily: "Yes, I have a message for Father Siemen."

"Sure, and you will enjoy yourself, young gentleman."

So mild was the day that the windows in the priest's house were flung open. I got there just as Father Siemen, his wife, and guest were sitting down to dinner, and so pleased were the priest and his wife with the prospect of an Easter present that a bowl of bean soup and some boiled fish were offered to me.

All manners forgotten, I stared at the visitor, a portly, florid man in a green coat and buff breeches, obviously an important relation because both host and hostess treated him with great deference. He ate much, and as he talked, I let my bean soup get cold, so entranced was I by his conversation. I can now suppose he was but a minor clerk in some government office, but his commissions often took him away from his desk and inkhorn. He mentioned places I had never heard of, he described meals in houses which made Bielogorka sink to the level of a peasant's hut, he talked of brigands he had captured and of murderers he had brought to the block. No doubt, much of it was colorful bragging, but how was I to know it? Having heard him, I felt as though I had drunk a goblet of very strong mead.

Then suddenly the fat man pushed his hand into his breast pocket, pulled out a crumpled half sheet of thick gray paper, and spread it on the table.

"That is one of the jobs I am saddled with." He spoke

importantly, and the priest and his wife leaned forward, amazement and servility stamped on their faces. "Yes," the fat man went on. "They tell me to go and find a girl run away from her parents' castle. I ask you! I dare say she fell for some good-for-nothing handsome young fellow with nothing but holes in his pockets. Yes, that is what comes of educating females," he wheezed. "What do you make of it, young man?" He turned to me.

I stared at the paper and shook my head.

"Well, you, not being a girl, should learn your letters some day," and he laughed and began moving a thick hairy forefinger under the first line of the writing. "Just listen." He read out very slowly: "Dear Papa and Mamma, Forgive me, I am happy. I will send word later. All is well with me. I must go. Mar—"

He threw back his head and grumbled.

"That chit was in such a hurry, she did not even finish her signature. Just 'Mar,' and her name is Maria."

The priest crossed himself. His wife gasped.

"Read it out again, cousin," she begged.

He did, and at that moment I knew that somehow or other I must get hold of the paper. The blood rushed into my face, but nobody noticed, and at that very moment the clerk's driver pushed his head through the door. One of the horses had a swollen fetlock.

"That is a job for Yanko," said the priest, and the two men went, leaving the paper on the table. I was all alone in the room, the priest's wife having gone to the kitchen. Suddenly a gust of wind shook the little house. I seized the paper, ran toward the church, and there, hiding the paper under my belt, bent my head and began searching. I heard the priest's wife call me, and I turned back, flushed and out of breath.

"That gust," I stammered, "it carried off your cousin's paper. I ran out to look and could not find it."

"What is there in a paper?" she said indifferently, and pressed me to have a piece of apple pie.

But I sat on tenterhooks until the priest and his cousin came back from Yanko's. Stumbling and stuttering, I told my story. The clerk shrugged.

"It does not matter, lad. I am sick and tired of the job anyhow, and nobody will ever find the girl. She is well over the Polish border by now, I reckon."

A little later, I was trudging back to Bielogorka. It never occurred to me at the time that my father, being illiterate, would ask either the priest or the deacon to read the message out to him. I thought of it just before I got home—but I felt I could trust the new priest and assured myself that the chances were the deacon had never heard about the paper.

And now it was late afternoon of Monday in Holy Week, the day on which I meant to leave Bielogorka. So warm and sunny had it been for some days that the last streaks of snow were gone from yard, garden, and field. That day my father kept me very busy in one of the outhouses sorting seeds, and I had no time to look my last at many of my favorite corners.

I did not really mind. Some people talk about feelings as though they were so many ripening pears on a tree—waiting to fall. I don't think they are right; feelings don't fall. But they lose their grip and strength, and they end by vanishing. I had no regrets whatever. I meant to get away and I also meant to succeed, some time, somewhere. There was no room for anything else in my mind. I had been afraid of my father since infancy, and I had great respect for my mother, but there had never been any affection on either side. To my father, Bielogorka and his horses came first. His children first and foremost belonged to the place and they had to justify their existence by doing anything the place demanded of them. We were not persons to him but so many pairs of hands and feet.

My preparations had been completed the evening before. A fairly capacious *kotomka* of stout sacking reinforced by leather thongs held a pair of breeches, my new boots, a couple of shirts, St. Mark's icon, a big hunk of cheese, a small rye *korovay,* and a piece of cold bacon. The gold piece and two *altinny*—each worth three kopecks—were sewn into my belt. Those coins had been hoarded by me for nearly a year. I believe they were given me by my father to buy a ribbon for Nastia!

A single candle burning in an iron stick on the table, we sat down to a meager enough meal of oatmeal soup and pickled herrings. There was bread but neither butter nor milk because my parents were strict about Lenten observances. I blushed as I drank my soup. I remembered the bacon and cheese in my satchel and I knew I would be a sinner long before the next sundown.

The last mouthful eaten, my father ordered Fenia and me off to bed. Both of us went up to the big chair, he made the sign of the cross over us, and we kissed his hand. Then, according to custom, we bowed to my mother and the servants. The day was over.

The Waiting Ends

Up in the loft, I settled down by my little window. I was determined to keep awake but I fell asleep until an owl woke me with a start. I rubbed my eyes hard and looked out the window. The somewhat tired light of the stars told me that it was time to go. The packed satchel, the old boots, and the sheepskins lay all ready to my hand. I tiptoed down the ladder into the kitchen. My father's loud snoring was the only sound in the house. I stole toward the table and laid the sheet of gray paper on it. Then very cautiously I made for the back door. Accustomed to the dark, I did not have to fumble for the latch, and I closed the door just as noiselessly.

It was bitterly cold. I slipped into my sheepskins, slung the satchel over my left shoulder, and got my boots on. Then I stood and listened, but the dogs never gave tongue.

I ran down the yard into the orchard and made for the great meadow, my heart beating fast. Presently, the splashing of the water reached me. I dived into my secret place and pulled out the little raft.

4

Those First Streaky Days

I had once imagined myself accustomed to space when covering the distance between my home and Malinovy. But, until that day in mid-April 1742, when, having crossed the Dnieper, I struck northwestward, I had not really known how vast the world was and how deserted it could be. Having climbed the steep bank, I found myself facing an enormous expanse of land, not a roof or a spire in sight. The ground was thickly dotted with low-grown prickly shrub, and here and there I saw straggling bushes of bearberry and a juniper or two. But there were no trees and, as the sun rose higher and higher, I had to shed my sheepskins. My *kotomka* grew heavier and heavier.

The vast common rose and fell, and the sight of a brook threading its way around the foot of a hillock filled me with rapture. I was on my way to a splendid future, the sun shone brightly, and I decided to have my first meal in freedom. Except for the very rare occasions when we would be banished from the house on account of some important visitor, I had never eaten alone. It was pure delight to do so, but I ate sparingly, aware that I must husband my resources. The world as I saw it seemed quite uninhabitable.

The sun was already dipping in the west when, the common left behind, I struck a path through a tangled coppice of thin larches. I came out into a field and saw a harrow in a corner. At the very end, a slim pencil of lilac-blue smoke was rising above the trees. Those, as I found, did not screen a village, not even a hamlet—but a mere huddle of some four or five huts sunk in little cherry orchards.

A friendly red-cheeked little woman stood there, two buckets swung on a yoke across her shoulders. Greetings were exchanged. She heard what I said and called out to her husband: "A bite and a sup and an armful of hay, master? The young one looks tired enough, and dusty, too."

The little man in a torn and stained blue *svitka* came out and grinned at me, and I felt I had acquired two friends in the strange world.

"Well." He tugged at his beard. "*Mozhe*—why not?"

It was a poor enough place, just a one-room hut with a brick stove, a table, a trestle, and some rough bedding lying along the wall. I was glad to be rid of my satchel and sheepskins, dropping them in a corner by the door. I washed the dust off my face and hands, and we sat down to sup off turnips boiled in water and a little salt fish.

"What will your name be?" asked the little man when we had eaten.

"Mark."

"And your father's surname?"

"Fedorov," I replied airily.

The woman wished to know where my home was, and when I said I lived near Kiev, she sighed and said they had never been across the Dnieper, and it rather comforted me.

"On a pilgrimage, I reckon?"

"Well, yes," I mumbled, and hoped they would not ask me which particular shrine I was making for, but the little man said: "To St. Andrew's by Mirgorod, I suppose? You are on the right road for it, lad."

I nodded. They yawned, and presently they bedded me in

fragrant hay in a barn, and I fell asleep at once. I awoke to a smiling golden dawn and my host standing in the doorway, his face purple with fury.

"Out with you, dirty infidel that you are!"

I leaped out of the hay as though it had scorched me.

"What do you mean?"

"Calling yourself a pilgrim in Holy Lent!" he blustered. "And carrying cheese and bacon for your victuals! No true Christian you are! Out I say!"

I should never have left my satchel in the corner of the hut. The dog had nosed it, bitten off one of the straps, and got at the bacon.

All the provender had been burned in the stove, the little woman said without looking at me, but they had left my clothing and the icon intact.

Between them, they hustled me off as though I had brought plague under their roof. They did not even offer me a mug of water, and the man wished me a bad Easter when I turned away.

Well, I had broken the church law by eating cheese and bacon in Holy Week. I had sinned and I had asked for something of the kind to happen to me, but I did not feel in the least ashamed of my sin. Lenten practices had always been incomprehensible to me. I could not see why it should please God to see His creatures stuffing themselves with fish, puddings and cakes made with honey (since sugar was forbidden), pulse, and all sorts of pies and pasties made with vegetable oil. Meat, poultry, cheese, butter, milk, eggs, and sugar—since animals' bones were used in the refining—were taboo. But the Lenten fare meant no sacrifice to the people.

They enjoyed it hugely, and so far as I remember, they would eat more in Lent than at any other time. It made no sense to me whatever.

It proved a hard day indeed. The season did not allow of any edible roots or berries. The sun was scorching. The wind died down. I trudged on, all sense of direction lost, across one vast common to another, and it was long past noon when, at the edge of a birch wood, I came on a brook. I drank my fill and felt better. The sun was just about to set when, having struggled through a wood, I came on a small camp of pilgrims seated by the fire lit by the bank of a narrow, sluggish river. I was famished and all but wondered whether my venture were doomed to end at no great distance from Bielogorka. But I saw a small white linen banner—a blue cross sewn on it—which stood against a fir, and I unbuttoned my shirt and pulled out my baptismal cross. That assured me an immediate welcome.

All of them, young and old, looked spent, and they did not talk much. But they gave me a bowl of vegetable stew and some bread, and let me sleep under a tree. At dawn, when they were getting ready to strike camp. I told them I was no pilgrim and that I was on my way to Moscow, where some of my kin lived.

"You make for Mirgorod, God's young man," said the eldest among them. "A lovely holy place Mirgorod is—nine churches, two monasteries, and four convents. You would not lack for bread there."

"Where is it?"

"Follow the sun," suggested a young pilgrim, but the others shook their heads.

"That would not get the lad to Mirgorod. You keep straight

on—an easy road it is, and a pleasant one—meadows and wooded hollows and a friendly hamlet or two. I reckon it is a three days' trek from here."

I offered them one of my precious *altinny*. They would not take it. They were generous. They promised candles and prayers at Korenna, and they filled my satchel with bread, dried fish and apples. All of them, about twelve in number, embraced me when I set out for Mirgorod with its nine churches, two monasteries, and four convents.

Now I cannot remember much of that very long trek to Mirgorod except that it took longer than three days and Easter was behind me when I reached the last lap—a gently sloping hollow fringed on one side by straggling elms and thorns, with a few little huts huddling together beyond the trees. It was still early afternoon but there had been no sun and a sharp north wind had been blowing since dawn. I had no idea how far I was from Mirgorod, and I hoped for some shelter in a byre or a barn. I had spent three nights in the open and my appearance was rather bedraggled, but that would not have mattered in the depths of the country.

I eased the satchel across my left shoulder and knocked at the door of the very first hut. It opened none too quickly. An ugly fat woman in a dirty green kirtle peered at me.

"Eh?" she mouthed in reply to my customary greeting— "Christ be with you." "And what may you be after?" she added, venom thickening in her voice. "We had two geese stolen yesterday. Well, what have you come for? From that fair, I reckon—thieves and vagabonds all of them!"

My heart beating rather fast, I stammered my request for shelter and a little food.

"I can pay," I added. "I am on my way to Mirgorod."

"A mere hour's tramp from here," she snarled at me. "Get you gone—else I'll loose the dog on you. But before you go, just tell me where my geese are."

I merely stared at her.

"I can see by your eyes that you are a thief and a vagabond," she rasped on. "Whom did you murder to get such smart sheepskins, ah, tell me that?"

I was petrified. I wanted to run away but I stood rooted. Her small brown eyes, thick bristles on her chin, her stained kirtle, her clenched fist—all about her was menacing. I cleared my throat once or twice but I seemed to have lost my voice. And we were just by ourselves. All the other folk of the hamlet must have gone off to the fields, spring sowing having begun.

She was still haranguing me when a young giant appeared from behind a clump of birches. He looked at me. He looked at her. He strode forward and in a trice the fat woman was inside the hut and the door slammed on her. Then he swung around and grinned.

"Been carrying on about the blessed geese, has she? They have just wandered down the stream—but she won't believe it, lad—she has had thieves on the brain all her life, my poor mother. Where are you off to?"

"Mirgorod," I stuttered.

"Well, you'll get there by sundown." He gave me simple enough directions. "Never been there myself for all it is so near. Too much incense about the place for my liking, but folks say the fair is good. You on a pilgrimage or what?"

I shook my head.

"Didn't think you were," laughed the giant. "You don't look the pious kind to me. Well, God be with you! Don't think ill of my mother—life's been hard enough for her."

"No," I murmured awkwardly, thanked him, and trudged off.

The afternoon was spent when I saw Mirgorod, the very first town in my life.

5

I Start a Career and Finish It

But I did not really see it, and I would soon leave its environs, all its churches, monasteries, and convents unvisited by me.

Between the town of noted piety and myself stretched a vast plain crowded with people and dotted all over with multicolored tents and gaily beflagged stalls. Horses neighed, people shouted and laughed, geese cackled, cattle lowed, dogs barked—wave upon wave of noise reached me as I stood at the edge of a small fir coppice. There were girls in embroidered kirtles, bright ribbons in their hair, women in scarlet and green kerchiefs, cossacks in white and blue *sharovary*, peasants in clean holiday *svitkas* embroidered in red at throat and wrists. I stared, having never seen so many people together in my life. The Malinovy fair was a dwarf's affair by comparison.

Here the wind veered and brought wafts of bruised grass, hair oil, sweat, honey, and roast meat together, and I realized how hungry I was. I moved forward, clutching one of my precious *altinny* in my hand. The crowds were so dense that it was quite a time before I could work my way to the nearest cook's stall. There I bought two slices of piping-hot roast mutton flavored with herbs, a sour-cream pasty, and a mug of

cider. The thin-lipped woman would not give me the change until I had finished eating and drinking. "Mugs can't be bought for a broken straw," she said. In the end I got two small copper coins as change for my *altinny*.

Then I plunged back into the crowds, nobody taking the least notice of me. I gasped and I gaped at all the unfamiliar sights—performing bears, fighting cocks, gypsies busily fortunetelling, Jews selling weirdly-colored medicines, a man who killed a mouse with his right hand and brought it out alive with his left, and many more. There was a sizable crowd in front of every entertainment tent.

Presently I got to the very end of the plain and saw a

shabby gray tent, no crowd outside. A fat little man in a faded red coat stood outside, tears running down his seamed cheeks and two thin shabby women were trying to comfort him.

"Never mind, Petra, you play a trick or two, and there is your trumpet."

"I did, and nobody wanted any of that," wailed the little man. "Dear wife, dear sister, you saw it yourselves. It is Semka they want. I am so ashamed. Never again do I come to Mirgorod fair. They would all say now: 'Petra Dikh is a cheat . . . Petra Dikh is a liar . . . Petra Dikh is no Christian!' All because I have shouted Semka's name all over the place. . . ."

"No, no," muttered the women.

So absorbed were they in their misfortune that they never noticed me.

"With a voice like his, those monks of St. Sabba's will never give him up," the little man wailed on. "Ah, Semka, Semka, the best songster from here to Chernigov."

"You are right there, Petra," said one of the women by way of comfort. "Those monks would as soon ride a cloud as give him up—but he went of his own free will, he did, Petra. . . ."

Having heard it all, I came forward, my mind made up.

"Sir, is it songs you want? I think I can sing."

The three stopped lamenting and stared at me in none too friendly a way. The women shrugged. Presently the fat little man muttered: "Well, come behind the tent, lad, and sing a verse of 'Over the Rapids'—that always fetches them. Mind, sing low."

When I had done, I saw the three of them exchange glances. The women kept silent. The fat man cleared his throat.

"You have got a bit of a voice," he said grudgingly. "Not like Semka's, of course, but a shrimp is better than no fish, as the saying goes." He paused, looked at the two women, and added carelessly, "Well, you might do worse than stay, lad."

"Stay?" I echoed.

"Yes, here, and then on to Poltava with us. A grand fair at Poltava, my lad, you will be rolling in butter and cheese."

But the mere name of Poltava made me shake my head. Nastia's mother lived near there, and my mother's cousins, too.

"I am making for Moscow," I said firmly. "I have kin there."

"In Moscow?" shouted the little man. "But it is just around the corner. Why, lad, you break your fast in Poltava and you dine in Moscow."

"Not as far as that," chimed in one of the women.

I did not believe them. I kept shaking my head. I had no intention of going to Poltava.

"I will help you out here till the end of the fair," I offered, and he replied somberly: "It is the last evening here. Ah well, a little finger is better than none. Now you keep behind me, lad, till I tell you to start. Know other songs, do you?"

"Oh, rather."

The younger of the two women told me where to leave my sheepskins and the satchel. I stood behind Dikh, my cheeks flaming and my hands icy. Supposing a crowd gathered outside and I could not sing. . . . But within an instant or two all nervousness left me, so absorbed did I get in the most wondrous fairy tale I had ever heard. Dikh's voice was like a trumpet. Standing there, his arms akimbo, the late afternoon sun turning his faded red coat into a garment of splendor, he shouted to all who cared to hear that he was fortunate to present to them a prodigy from Moscow, a lad with a voice like a silver bell mounted on gold, who had sung before no fewer than four archbishops, to counts and to princes all over the Empire. So outrageous and yet so oddly fetching was the story that quite a few loiterers left whatever they were looking at and moved nearer to Dikh's tent.

Dikh went on adding marvel to marvel for a few more minutes, and then beckoned to me to step forward.

"Give them 'Over the Rapids' to start with," he muttered.

I stepped forward, tried to smile, and took a deep breath. I sang "Over the Rapids," "The Cheery Orchard," the old Sword Song, a lullaby, the great favorite "Marussenka, Marussenka, where are the marigolds?," and one or two others. During the pauses I knew I was holding them, and I felt happier than I had ever felt before. I was dimly conscious that the few loiterers had grown into an oddly quiet crowd, and the hush deepened when, for a finale, I began the Cossack prayer:

> May my sword be never stainéd
> By a shameful thrust;
> May my oath be never broken—
> Death to foe, life for a friend.
> Christ, my Leader in the battle,
> This I pray of Thee;
> Holy Michael, the Archangel,
> Of thy valor give to me—
> That I fail not, that I struggle
> For the honor of our faith.

They did not clap. But as though from a distance I heard sighs and muffled sobbing. Presently muted voices rose to the pale green evening skies: *"Dobre! Dobre!"* "Good! Good!"

Adroitly, Dikh, an astrakhan cap in each hand, plunged into the crowd. I remained where I was, only half conscious of the surroundings. But I saw Dikh come back, the two caps filled to the brim with copper coins, silver glinting among them.

"Good, good," he muttered and edged past me into the tent.

Some time later, one of the women called me in for the evening meal. The food was good and plentiful and I would have enjoyed that super if it were not for Dikh's sour mood.

"So you won't stay?" he demanded, struck fire from his flint box, and lit his pipe.

"I don't think I can," I stammered.

He shrugged and left the tent. Somehow I did not wish to stay there with the two women. I followed Dikh.

"Please, sir, could I have my share now? I think I'd better get on."

"Your share of what?" He swung around and stared at me. "You are free to go, aren't you? I am not keeping you."

"Why," I gasped, "you had two caps full of coins—everybody gave something because I sang—"

I stopped. I could hear the two women's labored breathing behind me. The evening shadows were thickening and Dikh kept his face turned away.

"You did sing," he affirmed. "You offered to sing. You have had a good meal. I never promised you any money."

Then the blood rushed into my temples. I swung my right

arm and hit him. He staggered and I hit him again. A fat and flabby man, he was in no condition to fight, and I had him on the ground after the second blow. "You cheat and liar!" I shouted in my fury. "Get up this instant and fight me if you can."

Brawling was such a usual feature of every fair that nobody took the least notice of the scuffle. Certainly, nobody would have dreamed of interfering. Twilight was deepening, and flares were lit here and there, and I could hear a musician or two tuning their instruments. Dancing was about to begin. Here, quite inconsequentially, I remembered my satchel and sheepskins.

"I must get them out of the tent," I thought.

Dikh did not move. He lay on one side, his head turned away from me. The women ran up to him, and I heard him whimper that I had killed him and that he would have justice. I stooped for my things and ran, unaware of any direction, away from the flares and the stalls, when suddenly the giant figure of a cossack barred my way. His face I could not see. His white *sharovary* shone like silver.

"Let me go, please," I panted. "He asked for it—"

"He did, lad." The warm kindliness of the voice made me catch my breath. "Pity you did not finish him, the scoundrel, but he will never come here again. That Semka of his has not gone any monks. Dikh played the same trick on him. But, oh dear, lad, what a greenhorn you are! You should have asked for an earnest before you started," and, as he spoke, he began leading me back to the fairground. We passed Dikh's shabby tent, where, in the light of a flare, I saw him seated on the ground, drinking out of a mug. The two women shook their fists at me, and were it not for the burly cossack, I feel sure they would have pounced on me and torn at my hair. The cossack halted.

"Go back where you belong," he boomed at Dikh, "with thieves and scoundrels. If I see you about Mirgorod again, I'll break you bone from bone. Is that clear?"

His huge hand on my right shoulder, he led me away to a quiet corner between two stalls, and there he stopped.

"You fought well. You did not hit him again when he was on the ground. And you sang better. And what in the world are you doing near Mirgorod, Fedor Poltoratzky's son that you are? A good step from Bielogorka, isn't it?"

I shook so much that the satchel slipped off my shoulder. I did not pick it up. "So this is the end of it all," I thought wildly, when his deep voice went on: "Ran away from home, didn't you? I heard you singing. I knew you at once. You would not remember me. Time and again I have bought a horse from your dad. I know boys run away for a reason and sometimes without one. What was it that bit into you, lad?"

I breathed more easily. Somehow I knew that I could trust the stranger. The whole story came out, and he listened and never interrupted. When I had done, he said simply: "Well, now, I am on my way south. Happen I might make a halt at Bielogorka. What do I tell them?"

"That their son will try never to shame them," I gulped hard.

"I know that, lad."

"And—and—I hope they will forgive me. Sir, I couldn't help myself. Singing is all things to me."

"So it should be," he broke in dryly. "Know the way to Moscow, do you?"

"N—no," I stammered.

"Make for Korenevo when you leave here," and he plunged into terse, clear directions. "Tell Kuzma the smith that Ilyich the cossack sent you. He'll do what he can. God go with you, lad," and he stalked away and vanished among the crowds.

I liked him immensely, most of all for not offering me either money or shelter. I felt as though I had grown and matured within an hour. Ilyich the cossack left me to my adventure and he reaffirmed my faith in the outcome.

6

An Unexpected Interlude

I certainly owed a great debt to Ilyich the cossack because of an experience I had when I got to Korenevo.

I cannot remember how long it took me to get there. It proved a fairly long trek from Mirgorod, but the fine weather held. It was good to tramp through that lovely country, the little rivers gleaming like silver, the hamlets sunk in the crimson foam of ripening cherries, the golden cups of sunflowers upraised to the sun, the promise of a fair harvest brave and strong on every field of wheat and barley. As I got farther and farther from Mirgorod, I would come on bands of singing men and women busily scything and baling hay. There was no question but I must join them, a good supper my reward. Nobody thought much of my skill with the scythe, but the songs I gave them in the evening heartened them, so they said. Never once did I lack shelter or food.

It was fun to be up before dawn when the very air seemed young and to strike north again. It was fun to wash my clothes in one of the little rivers and to watch them dry in the sun, to gather wild berries by the handful as I ran through some wood. I walked barefoot just as I had done at Bielogorka, where boots were allowed in winter and for church only. Outside Romny I parted with a copper for a pair of bast sandals. I had never worn them before, but they proved a comfort when walking over many a rough patch. I sometimes remembered Petka's warnings about brigands, wolves, and bears—but such things, as I had reason to believe, belonged to the wintry season. Never a brigand did I meet, nor yet a wolf. Once in the distance I saw two bears, but they were busily stripping some wild raspberry bushes and took no notice of me. Otherwise, there were just friendly and overworked peasants, birds to listen to, and small beasts to make friends with. Hares were rather shy, but on many an occasion I would share a meal with a squirrel.

I had certainly learned much about distances since leaving Bielogorka. I knew that I would never reach St. Petersburg before the winter. I was determined to spend it in Moscow. Ilyich had mentioned Kaluga to me and said that a really good road ran from there to the old capital, and I had no doubt I would get to Moscow some time before the first frosts gripped the land.

And I think I might have done it if it had not been for Korenevo.

I found it easily enough. One or two people, of whom I asked directions, seemed rather startled at the name and answered with something of reluctance in their voices. But peasants are cautious folk and none would commit himself to a stranger.

So one sunny summer morning I halted at the top of a hillock studded with slim silver birches, and looked below.

An Unexpected Interlude

There ran the Seym, its banks enameled with blue, red, and purple flowers and its waters like a mirror. There stretched Korenevo, a tiny township rather than a village, every steading sunk in orchards, its wide curving street ending in a humpy wooden church with a squat blue cupola, the cross gleaming in the sun. Korenevo stood on the bank of the Seym—I could see flashes of water in between the little houses. I liked it at once, and wished it were in the neighborhood of Kaluga or, better still, Moscow. It seemed a comfortable place to winter in.

And then I noticed that the long street was empty. Neither man nor woman could be seen at any of the little gaily-painted gates. The fields away to the right—stretching into haze-veiled distances—seemed equally deserted, and that at the height of summer! I stared at the riverbank and I saw a crowd. For a moment I wondered if the entire population of Korenevo had gone mad: the crowd seemed so still and doing nothing at all. I had never seen an idle able-bodied peasant in my life.

Very cautiously I climbed down the hill and edged my way nearer and nearer. Nobody spoke. Nobody moved. I tugged at the sleeve of a lad about my own age.

"Sh-sh—" he muttered, his deeply tanned face looking as solemn as though we were in church. "Keep still . . . It is our *znakhar*, our medicine man, old Kostka. Laying the curse he is."

I edged my way around and around until I could see what was happening. Nobody took the least notice of me. We had a very skilled *znakhar* at Malinovy. The old man I saw seated

on the ground looked rather like a *koldoon* to me. His iron-gray matted hair brushed away from his forehead, his green eyes stared at the crowd as though they saw nobody at all, his sunken mouth kept moving soundlessly. Two bony hands were stretched over a weird collection spread on the ground between his feet: a dead cock, a bunch of elm twigs, some barley seeds, and a well-polished piece of a goat's horn. I knew it to be witchcraft—there was plenty of it in the neighborhood of Bielogorka, but never before had I met a man whose eyes saw you without looking at you. I can't explain it in any other way. I remember that I shivered once or twice.

Laying the curse, was he? To me it seemed as though he were doing the opposite.

Suddenly I heard a frantic mutter just behind me: "Father Pavel . . . Father Pavel coming—"

"Ah, Queen of Heaven, and we thought him away till tomorrow!"

"So he said—and Ozerovo is not around the corner—in a manner of speaking."

Everybody got as hurriedly busy as though the place were in flames. In a trice the cock, the elm twigs, and the rest vanished from the ground. Kostka, still seated, became absorbed in mending a fishing rod, and everybody turned his back on the river.

My godfather was a giant, but Father Pavel would have given him a few inches. The skirts of his gray linen cassock flapping in the breeze, he strode along, his blue eyes flashing with anger, his right hand clenched.

"What have you been at?" he thundered, and nobody answered him till an old woman said, rather foolishly: "Why, Father, we thought you were away—at Ozerovo."

"I know you did," he snapped, and then saw old Kostka. "And what have you been at? Muttering spells, eh?"

"Why, mending the fishing rod, Father," replied the old man in a high, shrill voice, the expression of his green eyes changed to perfect benevolence.

"I know some of the fishing rods you handle," shouted the priest. "You wait, old sinner! I will write to the bishop about you and your dealings with the devil. A stake or a gallows tree for you unless you mend your ways, do you hear? And all you folks should be at your work in the fields and the barns. A great calamity having fallen on Korenevo, it is at prayer you should be—instead of dabbling in witchery."

They listened, heads bent. The giant had done shouting, and they dispersed. Even Kostka shambled away, trailing the fishing rod behind him. The priest turned and stared at me hard.

"Where do you come from, lad?" he asked brusquely.

"From Mirgorod, Father."

"Know anyone in this place?"

I told him about Kuzma the smith.

"Gone to the heavenly kingdom last Lady-day," he replied, crossing himself. My face must have fallen, because he went on quickly: "Broken your fast yet? No? Well, come along then. There is always a bit of a sup for a stranger in my hut."

I thanked him and ventured to ask about the calamity. He tugged at his beard, and his face darkened.

"I'll tell you as we go along," he said.

It was a strange sickness among the livestock. Oxen, cows, horses, goats, all died of it, and nobody knew what it was. Pigs alone seemed immune. A beast would seem quite fit at dawn, then suddenly shiver as though its legs were made of straw, and foam at the mouth. Within a few minutes it would stagger down and die. With the harvest almost at the door, there was not a single horse left at Korenevo. All the carcasses having been burned and the ground well tarred afterward, the scourge, so the priest thought, should have left the place by now, and he had gone to Ozerovo to arrange for some horses and a few head of cattle to be sent to Korenevo.

"There are a few wealthy folk at Ozerovo," he explained, "and truly Christian they are. So the beasts will be here in a

70

day or two. But my people are so chickenhearted—terrified that the plague might return—so they get hold of that old warlock as soon as my back is turned, God forgive their foolishness."

I had seen some poor huts in my young life, but the priest's home seemed the poorest, and also the cleanest. It was just one fairly spacious room, a table and two trestles its only furniture. There was a homemade shelf for a few crocks, and some nails driven into the roughly timbered wall held little more than an extra cassock, breeches, and a kirtle or two. Some bedding lay on the floor underneath the shelf. The four icons in the east corner had no frames. But the two tiny windows shone and the white clay floor was as clean as newly fallen snow. As I remember it now, it seems to me that the Korenevo priest and his wife had turned their poverty into a thing of beauty.

The red-cheeked *popadia* looked something of a dwarf by comparison with her husband. She seemed quiet and kindly enough, but her speech told me that she was Russian and not Ukrainian. Not that she chattered. She set a wooden bowl with some stew on the table, a little bread, and, placing the wooden spoons in front of us, said briefly: "I am sorry their handles are broken."

"Well, their bowls are all right," retorted her husband.

We did not spend long over the meal, and there was not much conversation. On being asked my name, I gave that of Mark Fedorov. I quite expected further questions. None came.

Having had their bread and salt, I felt rather embarrassed. I knew only too well that they had shared what little there was. I could not offer any money as a return, but I felt I had to do something. Grace said, I turned to my host.

"Before I go on my way, I'd like to do you some service, Father," I offered shyly.

He gave me such a slap on the shoulder that I all but doubled up.

"Now, that is what I call a proper lad. Yes, son, there is something you can do. Any good at cleaning pigsties? Mine is a tiny one—just two pigs I have got—and they'll be out in the wood now, and I know it is time it were done—but what with the calamity and all!" He shrugged.

Now, the cleaning of a pigsty was not a job I excelled in, but I did not say so. The priest gave me a large pitchfork, led me to the tiny sty, and left me to it. I finished the job not too quickly since I had never learned how to handle either pitchforks or hatchets properly. My father could never understand it, since—with a good knife in my hands—I could turn out spoons, knife handles, and suchlike. But pitchforks, scythes, and hatchets seemed my enemies.

The pitchfork at Korenevo was no exception. A mistimed movement of my hands brought it sharply down on my right foot. One of the prongs tore through the bast of the sandal and blood gushed out. I bent down to look at it. It seemed an ugly enough jag, and I wondered whether the *popadia* could sell me a small piece of linen to bandage the foot when she happened to pass by the pigsty. She saw, put down the pitcher of water she was carrying, and beckoned to me. Then, quickly and silently, she washed the wound, tore up a handful of grass, kneeded it with her hands, and pressed it tight on the foot.

"That will stop the bleeding. Keep still for a bit." She picked up the pitcher and went off into the hut.

It certainly stopped the bleeding, but I could no more set out on my wanderings that day than catch at a cloud.

In the end, I was their most reluctant guest for more than a month. They bedded me in a small barn at the back of the hut. The village folk, overjoyed by the arrival of some livestock from Ozerovo, vied with one another in trying to lighten the priest's burden by leaving varied offerings at the door. The *popadia* was grateful. Father Pavel, once the callers were out of earshot, would say with a wry smile: "Well, Mark, that is what comes of being a stranger. It is hard work and all to get my tithe out of them—let alone presents."

For about ten days I could not move easily but hobbled about with the help of a stout ash stick. That pitchfork had been vicious indeed and the jag had run deep. I had my knife and asked the priest to get me a few pieces of limewood. I believe I carved enough spoons and knife handles to last their lifetime. I was as busy as I could be, but I did not sing at Korenevo.

I had not the least reason for thinking such things—but I did not feel at ease with my host and hostess. They were certainly kindly and generous, too, but I could not escape a feeling that they were puzzled about me. I should not have blamed them for it, but I did. The priest wanted to know which among Kuzma's kin had sent me to him, and such curiosity was but natural, but the simple question made me blush.

"Not a relation, just a friend, Father."

"And you are off to Kaluga now?"

"Yes, and then on to Moscow."

"A good step from here. Got any kin in Moscow?"

"Oh yes." I bent my head over the piece of limewood I was turning into a trencher.

"Where do they live?" Father Pavel added, still further deepening my confusion. "I went there once as a young man, son."

"By St. Barbara's," I said at random.

"Now, which St. Barbara's?" he wanted to know. "There are three or four of them."

"St. Barbara's of the Miracle," I said, having just remembered my brother Mikhail talking about some such church in Kiev.

Father Pavel shook his head slowly.

"I can't remember that one. Is it near the Yauza bank?"

"Yes."

"It must have been built since my time," he mused. "Not a single St. Barbara's on either bank of the Yauza do I remember. Well, lad, is it an uncle or just a kinsman you are going to?"

"An uncle," I replied quite wildly.

"And what does he do?"

"He is a farrier."

He knit his bushy eyebrows. "Well, you are a bit old to be an apprentice, lad, aren't you?"

"I am not going to be a farrier, Father," I answered. "I–I work on the land really. It is just a family matter. See, my uncle has no children."

"Ah, going to adopt you he is, isn't he?"

"No," I said, aware that I was getting rather too near very thin ice.

"Making you his heir then?" decided Father Pavel. "And what does your father do?"

"Oh, he just works a bit of land," I answered, shamelessly reducing Bielogorka to the level of a peasant's holding.

There were endless other questions, all asked quietly and good-naturedly, but each day I felt as though I were tying myself up into more and more knots. There was that Uncle Matvey in Moscow, and I had to remember that he was a farrier and not a baker, that he had no children, that he lived somewhere near St. Barbara's of the Miracle. That fabled uncle cost me many a sleepless hour.

Now you may wonder why I did not feel at my ease with either Father Pavel or his *popadia*. They were so kindly and certainly would have helped me in any way to them possible. But I did not need help, I said to myself, and to open my secret to them would have meant running into danger. Father Pavel had threatened the old warlock with the bishop and someone very high up in Kiev. Those words had made me realize that he, though a penurious parish priest, knew important folk and could get in touch with them. I had not been in his hut a week before I knew that he was a zealot in the cause of the Church. Had he as much as got a vague idea of the gift I so treasured, he would at once have decided that I must spend my life singing to the glory of the Lord and the Church, and—like old Father Foma at Malinovy—would have imagined me in full archdiaconal panoply. But, wholly unlike Father Foma, Father Pavel had drive in him. He would have persuaded, argued, cajoled, and probably forced me in the end to accept a life I knew was not for me.

It was well into the Little Assumption Lent in August when my foot mended and I could leave Korenevo. It fell on a very hot morning. We broke our fast hurriedly. The *popadia* filled my satchel with bread, cheese, and bacon, and Father Pavel gave me his blessing. Then, towering over me, he looked at me in silence, and in a flash I knew that he did not believe at all in that farrier uncle in Moscow near St. Barbara's of the Miracle. He did not say a single word, but I blushed to the very roots of my hair and again stammered my thanks for the directions he had given me the night before.

For all the kindness I had had, it was a relief to leave Korenevo.

I can remember no names along the next lap of my wanderings. There must have been a good number of them because, as I was to learn later, it proved an exceptionally long lap. The heat still held by daytime, but nights were getting fresher and fresher, and my sheepskins did not protect my legs. Some of the barns where I would be given shelter happened to have a horsecloth or two lying in a corner. Elsewhere, I would bury my body deep in the hay, which was fragrant and warm, but not always warm enough.

Then one morning, about a fortnight or so after leaving Korenevo, I said goodbye to my host and left that very tiny poor hamlet. Once I was well across the field, I halted and sniffed. There was rain in the wind.

That summer had been checkered by numberless showers which would come and go and leave you refreshed in every muscle of your body. But that morning the wind held no promise of a swift shower. The skies were deceptively blue— scumbled here and there with milky white drifts of clouds; yet I did not like the way a row of aspens was bending to the wind, and at a distance I saw a hare running, its ears pressed back, which in my country was always taken as a sign of breaking weather.

However, it did not break that day or for some days to come.

And then came a morning which was not really a morning, for all the light you could see. The night had been astonishingly warm, and I had spent it in a tiny hollow along the edge of a wood. I woke up and rubbed my eyes. Overhead, the skies were the color of blueberry soup. I scrambled out of the hollow and listened. The whole world lay still. The air seemed to have turned into a curtain of thick gray silk. Not a leaf stirred, not an animal footfall was heard. I had a little food in my satchel, but I forgot my hunger. I knew that the storm would break any minute. The little wood was behind me and I might have found shelter there. But my thoughts were all in a maze. I took to running across a vast space in front of me, all sense of direction out of my mind. There seemed no other sound left in the world except the beating of my heart.

I cannot remember how long I ran. I halted, shifted my gear from one shoulder to another, and mended my pace. Presently, a streak of pale gray-blue broke across the sky, to be followed by another and yet another. The world was just as uncannily still, but the sight of the skies certainly heartened me. I sat on a tree stump and had a little food, and then trudged on. I had a vague sense that I should not have been walking away from that hollow, but I comforted myself by the thought that the folk in the next hamlet would put me on the right way again.

The next moment the storm was on me. I had spent my life in the country and known many a wild tempest, but nothing as furious as what I met that day. The sudden wind smote at me with a hundred flails. The gray silk curtain of the air turned to sheer black. Out of the inky darkness came the heavenly floodgates. Within a moment I was soaked to the skin. That on its own would not have troubled me at all. What shredded my courage was the fact that I, accustomed to finding my way on a moonless night, could see nothing at all. The dark was impenetrable. Doubled up by the wind, I struggled ahead.

I never heard the thunder, but a tremendous flash of lightning showed me a coppice at no great distance ahead. I made toward it, my confused thoughts running on: "A wood starts here . . . It must end somewhere . . . Everything must end . . . I'll shelter there . . . Beyond may be a village, or a heath, or a mountain—but something—I don't care what—and this rain can't go on forever. . . ."

Well, it was a small coppice and I plunged in. At that moment the wind went down, and I heard a crash somewhere near. It seemed odd that the crash should have started squeezing my breath out of me. I cannot remember falling. I do remember closing my eyes because one part of my body was just a knot of burning pain. "I cannot be in Paradise," I thought dazedly, "because there is no pain there."

How long was it before I opened my eyes again? I cannot

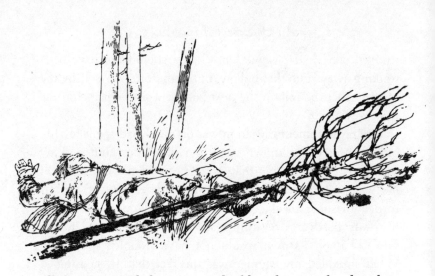

tell, but I opened them to see the blue skies overhead and to feel a very gentle breeze fanning my face. I lay on the ground, and I could see the slim trunk of a young fir across my left foot. I knew I could not move, and my first thought was a foolish one: "I have always loved firs. . . . Why should one of them have hurt me so?" Then I closed my eyes again.

It was some time later that I knew I was not alone. I no longer felt any weight on my left leg, and there were voices. I lay still, my eyes closed.

"Is he dead, Father?"

"No, no, he is breathing all right. Such a comely lad, too. Now shift him a bit, brother. That will do, that will do—"

The pain rose to such a peak that I must have screamed.

"Steady, lad, steady." A rough, calloused hand began stroking my hair.

A younger voice asked, "Shall I carry him, Father?"

"No. You run back and ask Father Iona for a cart and lots of hay, and I'll stay here. Mind you be quick, brother."

An Unexpected Interlude

There were no more voices. I opened my eyes. I saw a very old, frail monk, his habit shabby and his pink face creased with anxiety. He saw me look at him and bent over me.

"Never mind, lad. Any broken bone gets mended in time, the Lady be praised."

I must have lost consciousness again. I came around when clumsy unaccustomed hands began lifting me off the ground. I opened my eyes and saw the smiling blue skies. They seemed so oddly near that I thought I could touch them by raising my hand. But I did not want to move even my little finger. I said loudly and clearly, "Please, am I on my way to Moscow?" I heard the old man mutter, "Bless my soul! The lad is wandering," and I knew no more.

7

The Future All but Snatched from Me

Now I feel sure those monks did it all for the best, the best as
they knew it to be for themselves, and the best as they
thought it would be for me. Yet through that very long winter
spent neither at Kaluga nor in Moscow but behind the tall,
spiked walls of Surazhy Abbey, I was certainly nearer despair
than I had ever been before, my ambition turned into a
handful of shriveled yellow leaves at my feet.

There were many monasteries in the neighborhood of
Malinovy, but my father did not care for monks and none
would ever call at Bielogorka, so that I knew nothing whatever about the kind of life they led. By the time I had spent a
few weeks at Surazhy, I knew it to be a place where bells rang
precisely at the same time during night and day, where silence
was kept not only within the house but outside, and where
black-habited men were engaged in activities which—to my
mind—had nothing to do with religious life. I had imagined
such people to spend their whole days in church. In reality,
the monks of Surazhy were fishermen, husbandmen, lumber-
jacks. They had horses and a big herd of cattle. Away from
the monastery buildings stretched a long row of workshops.
Practically everything used at the abbey was made by the

monks' own hands—from a cartwheel or a horseshoe to a wooden platter. They also brewed beer and sold it. So much land was theirs that a good harvest brought a surplus of corn, and that, too, would be sold. Hardly a day passed but the big iron-barred gates would swing open to admit portly blue-coated merchants come to purchase timber, corn, untanned hides, even honey and mushrooms.

It was a great hive, but the cliff-like stone wall, studded with iron spikes at the top, which surrounded the abbey proper all around, was rather frightening.

They had brought me into a small ground-floor cell and there nursed me roughly but effectively, and within a few weeks my trouble had mended. It grew chilly out of doors and bitterly cold in the stone-walled cell, which had no other furniture but the pallet I slept on. There was a large window giving out onto the yard and, by raising myself on an elbow, I could see the corner of the church and the great gates in the distance. Three times a day an elderly monk with a mole on each cheek brought the food—a little fish, some boiled root vegetables, rye bread, and water in a crock. On Sundays I would have an apple or a handful of nuts. The man smiled, patted my shoulder, wished me good health, but never lingered. There was also the infirmarian, Father Matvey, still young, with a long red beard. He, too, was kindly, though his hands were somewhat rough.

But those two and some others whom I was to meet later remained remote.

Father Iona did not. He was the treasurer, a small fat man with an untidy grayish beard and small brown eyes which made me think of gimlets. He and Father Hyacinth, the choirmaster, came almost every day. Hyacinth's visits were of the briefest. But Iona would sit down on the floor, tuck his habit under his legs, and then begin spreading the blanket of his curiosity all over the cell until I felt I could hardly breathe for the confusion his questions threw me into. Of course, it was stupid of me to get so frightened. The monks had rescued me and were nursing me back to health. It was only natural that they should know something about a stranger. So I realize now. But I did not at the time. I felt myself in a trap. Of course, Iona wanted to know where I had come from.

"Mirgorod."

"Why"—he pulled at his beard, his sharp eyes never leaving my face for an instant—"it is a good step from here."

I said nothing.

"Where do you belong, son?"

"Oh, Lebedina, across the Dnieper," I replied, the name of the village some distance away from Malinovy having just slipped into my memory.

"Would it be a village now, or a small town?"

"It is a hamlet."

"And what made you take to the road then—and where are you making for?"

"Moscow." I slid past the first of the two questions, and then very slowly and carefully repeated the story about that imaginary uncle in Moscow. When I had done, I realized that my face was flaming.

Like the priest at Korenevo, Iona did not believe any of it. Unlike that priest, he said so.

"Well, son, soon, as Father Matvey tells me, you will be up and about. When things are right with you, you will tell me the truth."

"But I have told you the truth," I mumbled.

Iona's eyes narrowed into slits, but their stare remained as sharp as ever.

"You don't look like a farrier's nephew to me. Your speech is not that of a peasant. Mark Fedorov you said your name was, didn't you? Well, Mark, we are all God's men here and we don't hound God's creatures, whatever they may have done. Are you on the run?"

In my turn I stared back at him.

"Killed anyone or what?"

Swiftly I remembered Petka Dikh in Mirgorod, whom I might have killed, but I did not mention him. I replied defiantly: "By the Cross, I have neither killed nor robbed anyone."

Iona got up, stroked his beard, and spoke weightily: "Now this time I think I can believe you, lad."

Then he took his eyes away from me and asked almost casually, "Anyone taught you your letters?"

"No."

"What are you good at?"

"Well, I can carve things and cook, too, a bit." I hesitated. "And I have worked on the land."

"Ah," said Iona in a fatly satisfied voice. "Your father's land, would it be?"

"He owns an acre or two."

After that interview I made a vow: not a soul at Surazhy was to know about my voice. I knew I would have to spend the winter there, and I supposed it was my duty to earn my keep. Well, said I to myself, I would carve all manner of things, dig, chop wood, help in the kitchen, anything at all, and I would keep dumb at work. Then the spring and the open spaces again, Kaluga, Moscow, and the north.

Iona went on visiting me but there were no more "inquisitions." He would talk about the abbey, its long history, the sieges it had withstood—fighting Pole, Lithuanian, and even Tartar. The past of Surazhy certainly explained those high walls, but nothing I heard lessened the feeling that they were prison walls.

When Hyacinth started teaching me the alphabet, and the use of the abacus, I guessed that they had a plan for me, its details known to none but themselves. Certainly I was eager to learn and I learned quickly, but my suspicions deepened when to a question—"Why should you spend so much trouble on me?"—Hyacinth, stroking his cadaverous yellow cheeks, replied ambiguously: "Enlightenment brings great advantages, son." And he added: "You are a promising pupil indeed."

I must have been. By the time Christmas came, I was able to read any book Hyacinth gave me, and I felt perfectly at home with the abacus.

He never asked awkward questions and I would have liked him, had it not been for my deepening suspicions. Tall and thin, he had the blue eyes of a dreamer and a peculiar silken voice. But he glided rather than walked, a switch tucked through his leather belt.

My recovery accomplished, I still slept in the same ground-floor cell, but now they started working me hard, always in company with about a dozen gawky young novices, whom I did not get to know at all since all speech was forbidden during work and I never saw them at any other time. I sawed

logs, helped in the carpenter's shop, chopped root vegetables in the kitchen, swept snow, and continued having my lessons with Hyacinth. I went to Mass and Vespers but not to other offices, and was on my feet all day long. In church, if anyone as much as leaned against a pillar, Hyacinth would creep from behind, the switch in his hand, and the switch certainly hurt. The fare was poor and scanty, and the innumerable fast days were all but unbearable. More than once, having helped in the kitchens, I would tiptoe my way into one of the larders, snatch at whatever seemed most handy, and gobble it up in the darkest corner I could find.

There are good monks and bad monks all over our country, and I think that Abbot Piemen was the best among the good. For some time I had felt that neither Iona nor Hyacinth trusted me. When, just at the beginning of Lent, I was summoned to the Abbot's rooms, I said to myself, "I have heard that he is a good man—but I must be careful, even with him."

The Abbot had been ill and I had not seen him before—not even in church. A tiny man, he looked so frail that it seemed as though a light breeze would carry him off. The room was as hot as a bathhouse, but the hand I kissed was as cold as ice. Yet there shone warmth in the sunken gray eyes, and when I heard him speak, I felt as happy as though I were listening to a nightingale in a summer wood. He beckoned me to a stool near his armchair, and said very softly: "You are quite well now, my son?"

"Oh yes, Father Abbot."

One tiny hand, its skin the color of very old ivory, began fingering his amber beads. The gray eyes looked at me, and theirs was a look to open a window, to unlock a door, to enable one to wing one's way far, far away.

"I am glad," the soft voice went on. "You have a difficult time ahead of you, my son, but I see a golden gateway at the end." Suddenly I knew there was nothing for me to tell him—the old man could read my thoughts. And the knowledge did not frighten me because I knew I could trust him.

He went on more and more slowly, so tired he was: "You carry a great secret, Mark, and you must keep it a secret for some time. Don't be afraid. God has blessed you so far and He will bless you to the end." The voice sank to a barely audible whisper. "Be true to your great gift. Go in peace and pray for me, sinner that I am."

I was never to see him again. Even at the time he no longer governed the abbey, Iona being his deputy. Once outside that overheated room, I stood lost in thought and in wonder also. That brief meeting with Abbot Piemen had given me courage to carry on—in spite of everything.

And I came to need courage very badly within the next few days.

One morning during the second week of Lent, Mass finished, we broke our fast in the gloomy, vaulted refectory. So cold was it that my teeth chattered against the rim of my bowl. I was to sweep snow later on in the morning and the prospect cheered me up—that was warming enough work.

Alas! No sooner was I out of the refectory than Hyacinth summoned me to have a lesson. He would be busy with the choir in the afternoon, he said, adding, as he leafed the huge pages of Simeon Polotzky's treatise on faith, "By the way, Mark, come spring, I must try your voice."

I shook my head.

"I have no ear at all," I stammered.

"Ah well, we can soon find that out," he told me.

I read a whole page of Polotzky. I managed to solve two sums, and I recited a short psalm from memory. I was just finishing when Iona appeared. Hyacinth and I got up. Iona made a small gesture to the choirmaster, who bowed and left the room.

"Now, what's coming?" I wondered to myself. "I did

steal three soused herring last night, but nobody saw me."

Iona never hurried. He settled himself down on a bench, crossed his fat hands in his lap, and looked at me hard.

"You saw Father Abbot a few days ago?" he asked unnecessarily, since he knew all about it.

"Yes."

"He is a true saint," went on the treasurer. "Still in the flesh, he is also in heaven. He can read people's thoughts. He can see into the future. But his days are numbered, Mark, his days are numbered."

It was quite an effort to hide my panic. I stood in silence.

And Iona was very clever at gauging the length of a pause. It was quite a few moments before he began again.

"Well, Mark, we nursed you, taught you letters, bedded you, and fed you." Again he paused, and I thought to myself that I was more than earning my meager keep. "Therefore you are in our debt, my son."

I blushed and stammered: "Surely I can work it off?"

"Oh yes," he blandly agreed. "But is it not for the creditor to decide the means whereby a debt should be settled? It is a very big debt, Mark. Why, you might have died if our people had not rescued you in that wood."

There was nothing to say to that and I said nothing.

"You are a lad of great parts," he went on. "Father Hyacinth tells me he has never had such a pupil. You are good at letters and you are good at a great many other things. I am not saying it just to puff up your vanity but to make you see that every gift should be used for the greater glory of the Lord within His Church." He paused and I clenched my fists very hard. He glanced at my hands and smiled gently. "Don't look as scared as a hunted leveret, my son. The Lord does not compel. He invites—though it is hard going for such as refuse the invitation. That would cancer the soul," he said very slowly, every word minted as harshly as though it were of iron. "Surazhy needs lads like you, Mark, and you are just about the right age for the novitiate. That will be a fine and an honorable way to discharge your debt to us. Indeed, we think it the only way."

I stared at him blindly and stuttered, "Father Abbot—"

"Father Abbot," Iona broke in gently, "does not govern this house any longer. I am in his place, Mark. Anyway, we expect his departure almost any day now."

We were in Hyacinth's meagerly furnished office, but I saw neither the table nor the benches. I saw nothing but the cliff-like walls studded with iron spikes and the enormous barred gates. I was almost fighting for breath.

"I have no call for such a life—none at all—"

"We think differently, Mark."

"And my people—" Here I broke off, and again Iona smiled.

"We'll talk about your people later on, son. There is time between now and Easter Day."

"Easter Day—"

"Yes, a fine day to start the novitiate, Mark, isn't it?"

"No," I shouted, clenching and unclenching my fists. "Never, never!"

Iona's pudgy hand tugged at his belt and I quite expected the switch to fall across my shoulders, but he did not hit me this time. He merely told me to sweep the snow during the dinner hour.

"Hard work," he said unctiously, "is the best fare for a proud stomach."

The cook, however, took pity on me, and, the snow swept, I hid myself in a corner of a barn and there chewed a cold cabbage pasty and a couple of apples.

I had hoped to leave Surazhy with my satchel—so honorably left untouched in my cell—slung over my shoulder, all the farewells exchanged, my gratitude expressed and their blessing given. But now I knew that such a manner of departure was out of the question. I was very ignorant of the Church law and had no idea whether or not the monks were within their rights to make me a member of their house. In any case, Iona would have got two or three others to swear they had heard me promising to join them, and how was I to know that such a promise would not be binding? Moreover, for all my ignorance, I knew that once I was turned into a novice, I could never leave. I had heard quite enough stories about grim penalties meted out to deserters from monastic houses.

It was bleakly obvious that they had made up their minds to have me, and I had an uneasy sense that Iona knew much more about my antecedents than he let out. Merchants came and went often enough, and how was I to tell if any among them did not come from my part of the country? My father being a man of substance, some portion of it could be claimed by the abbey.

"I must escape," I said to myself and, leaving the barn, glanced toward the walls. My heart sank. I might manage the climb—but those wicked spikes would certainly defeat me. As to the huge gates—and they were the only ones—they were barred and padlocked at Vespers. They faced the yard, which was never wholly deserted. There was always a watchman or two, usually elderly, grave monks. Flight by day seemed impossible. Flight by night—equally beyond my reach.

That evening, alone in my cell, I forgot the bitter cold. I was just a lump of misery.

Easter fell late that year, and by mid-Lent breaths of spring could be felt out of doors, but for the first time in my life I was not conscious of the year's renewal. When working in the great kitchen-gardens to the west of the church, I would sometimes raise my head and scan that terrible wall, and there was nothing for comfort to see.

I was baffled that neither Iona nor Hyacinth ever spoke to me about the future again. In fact, I saw less and less of them as the days went on. The old Abbot died on the fourth Sunday in Lent, and all the senior members of the house were busy with the coming election soon after Easter. From the few cautious remarks I overheard when at work, I gathered that Abbot Piemen's successor would be none other than Iona.

I heard it and remained indifferent. Nothing seemed to matter any more.

The spring slush had passed, and we reached Passion week. It was about then that I noticed they were watching me. Once I halted near the open gates to stare at the pale brown buds of a chestnut outside, and one of the watchmen said quietly: "Now then, lad, get you away from here."

And there were many other similar incidents. We sometimes went outside the abbey grounds, right into the fields and I knew that one man of our company had been instructed to keep an eye on me.

It fell on the morning of Saturday just before Palm Sunday. I had some job or other to do in one of the workshops on the north side of the great yard. Suddenly a fearful commotion broke out. I left my tools on the bench and tiptoed to the half-open door. I saw Iona and one or two other monks facing a tall man in a bright blue coat and snow-white *sharovary*. He looked affluent, sure of himself, and burningly angry.

He roared at the monks: "Never do I buy a rotten bean from you again, do you hear? I don't owe you a penny, the saints be my witnesses! I came here last Michaelmas. Hemp, honey, hides, everything was paid for on the nail. From Moscow to Kiev you would not find a more honest merchant than Kondraty Kolubin."

He stopped to draw a breath, and Iona shouted back: "If you paid, where is the receipt? Seventy-nine rubles you owe us."

"Never a kopeck," stormed the man. "You said you would give the receipt next time I came. I should never have trusted you, Judases that you are, every one of you! Think a *klobuk* can cover up everything, do you? Never a copper do you get out of me for what I had here at Michaelmas."

Here an elderly monk whose name I did not know said mildly: "Now, my good sir, it is hardly seemly to shout like that within these walls, God forgive you!"

"I will not be called a cheat by anyone," roared "the good sir," his face crimson with fury.

Iona bent forward. "And nobody has used such a word," he said conciliatingly. "Father Seraphim is right. Come to the guest house, have a hot bath and a good dinner. Later—with God's blessing—we may find a way out of the wood."

"Leave me be," retorted the man. "I know my way about

the place. And you need not look like frightened hares—I am not going to set fire to your place. Just let me alone, will you?"

The monks moved away, and so did I from my coign of vantage. I felt most wickedly happy. Never before had I seen Iona or Hyacinth in such a predicament. I was certain they had cheated the merchant, and I liked the man. He may well have boasted about his high repute, but there was such a sense of freedom about the man, I felt that I could trust him through thick and thin. I wished I might be able to speak to him, and how could I? The guest house was out of bounds for me. I went back to my tools, and within a few moments I heard a voice at the door. There he stood, arms akimbo, peering into the shed.

You either trust a man or you don't. And I trusted Kolubin from the moment I saw him.

"You a novice or what?" he barked at me.

I shook my head. He shrugged, turned away, and then came back and peered more closely.

"You don't look the stuff they are made of." He spoke weightily. "Do they lodge you at the guest house or where?"

Eyes bent, I told him where my cell was. He said nothing. He turned away, and I finished what I was doing and went to my dinner.

I did not know what I was eating and I cannot now remember what I worked at through the afternoon. The sun had gone behind the clouds, but everything seemed golden to me because hope was breathing once again. There was not the least reason why I should hope at all—the man had attracted me but he was a stranger. Having quarreled with the monks, he would be unlikely to visit Surazhy again and, for all I knew, he would leave at dawn. Neither his *kibitka* nor his horses were seen in the abbey grounds. I could not even tell that he was spending the night at the abbey, and the scene in the yard considered, that did not seem likely. None the less, I hoped, and went on savoring the words he had spoken to me in the workshop.

It being a fast day, there was no supper, but I noticed that all the senior monks went to the chapter house once Vespers were over. That, I knew, meant a long session behind closed doors.

Now the cell allotted to me was in a small two-storied building jutting out at right angles from the church. Mine were the only quarters there. All the other rooms both on the ground floor and above were store places. I used to feel a bit lonely there sometimes: monks and novices' dormitories were some distance away, the Abbot's lodging still farther. The great yard remained wholly deserted after the Silence bell, and everything kept eerily still until some time after midnight, when candlelight began flickering in the church windows and the Matins bell began summoning the community to the longest Office of all.

That evening I could not sleep and sat by the window. The chapter-house lights had long since gone out. Everything would have been still if it were not for the wind whispering in the trees. Then I heard a cautious footfall and saw the flicker of a lantern. My heart all but missed a beat. I crept away from the window and waited.

In a moment or two Kolubin was in the cell.

"I told you I knew my way about." He did not trouble to

speak in whispers. "All the sanctified beards are safely asleep, I reckon." He put the lantern on the floor and lowered himself on the pallet. "Well, lad, I have learned a thing or two about you today. The holy fathers think they've got a nice fat fish into their net—what with the portion your family is sure to give you, and all your own gifts."

"They know nothing about my family," I began, and he chuckled.

"Ah, Queen of Heaven, I haven't known them for nothing come twenty years next Assumption Day. That fat Iona would beat a mole at underground work. A question here, a question there, and he puts everything together, and an angel from heaven would not be able to tell how two and two can make five!"

"I did not answer his questions."

"He would not ask them of you, lad. Merchants come here from all sorts of places, some as far as Kiev, others from Poltava. And I know my kind—we know how to keep our own counsel and we also know how to gossip. Ukraina is big enough but gossip does travel. Seven-league boots it wears, lad. So fat Iona has discovered that you have a brother at Pechera Abbey, and he knows too whose son you are."

"My father," I spoke through clenched teeth, "will never consent—"

"And will they bother about his consent once you are properly noviced? No, lad, I know the law, and so do the holy beggars here. But don't let us waste time on them. I mean to get you away from them, see?"

For a moment I wondered if the little cell were unwalling itself.

"Why?" I brought out huskily.

"Well, partly because Kondraty Kolubin likes to get his own back. They have cheated me all right. I know I did pay them in the autumn, but there is no proof, and I have to pay again. And that would make it nicely square between us. I like keeping tidy accounts, lad. Next, well, I like what little I have seen of you. Is that enough?"

I muttered, "Sir, they keep a watch on me by daytime when the gates are open."

"I'd have as much sense as an aspen leaf if I tried to get you away by daylight," Kolubin broke in. "Are you good at climbing?"

I remembered the cliff-like wall and said, "Well, yes, trees and riverbanks—"

He nodded.

"The wall is spiked," I went on, rather woodenly.

"I'll see to the spikes," he broke in. "Now, lad, it must be next Monday. You keep awake till the Matins bell, and when it stops, make for the kitchen-garden—know where that is?"

I nodded. I had often worked there.

"Mind you bring your gear and walk softly in case the dogs hear you. Make for the middle buttress—I have counted them—the middle one is the seventh from the corner. Whistle, but not too loudly, and leave the rest to God's mercy and my cunning."

He picked up the lantern and was gone before I could say a word.

Not that I had anything to say. I was confounded, happy, and fearful all at once. I suppose I fell down on the pallet and slept. I cannot remember. And there came Sunday. It passed, and so did Monday. I had not seen either Iona or Hyacinth. On Monday evening I went back into my cell. My little satchel was packed. I settled down by the window, resolved not to sleep, but I must have dozed off because the Matins bell startled me. I waited, my cold hands clutching the satchel. The bell stopped and I slipped out. Soon enough I came to the kitchen-garden, made out the seventh buttress, halted, and whistled.

Silence answered me. I tried to assure myself that there was no hurry—the Office would take more than two hours. None the less, despair brought tears to my eyes. How could I gauge the time? Was it the right evening? Had Kolubin changed his mind? Somewhere far behind a dog barked, and I froze.

Then I heard a whisper from the other side of the wall.

"You there, Mark?"

"Yes," I gulped.

"Now keep still."

I heard a sound suggesting that iron was being scraped against stone. In a moment or two I saw what looked like a ladder swung toward me.

"See it? Can you?"

"Yes."

"Catch hold of it before it touches the ground. Then up you get!"

I waited. I climbed. My feet on the last rung, I peered right and left, and heard Kolubin's voice.

"My man and I got two spikes out each side. You are safe. Not much of a drop, and the grass is soft."

I took a deep breath, released my hold on the ladder, and jumped. He helped me up.

"Not hurt, are you?"

"No," I gasped.

"Well, I am glad. We've got a fairly long lap to cover, lad. I could not risk bringing the horses anywhere nearer. Those dogs would have stirred the dead."

"The ladder—" I muttered, and Kolubin laughed.

"Just a keepsake for the holy fathers. . . . They can't claim you now, you know."

We were striding along a dark world, but all seemed light to me, and I began humming.

"Why, lad, can you sing?"

I answered with a gay cossack ballad. Kolubin said, "You would put a nightingale to shame, lad."

I was too happy for words. I tramped on and on. Presently a shape loomed out of the dark, and Kolubin called out: "Here we are, Timoshka! I've settled with the holy fathers all right. Lend a hand, will you?"

Someone hoisted me up. I smelled apples, spices, and leather. I knew everything was all right, and I knew no more.

8

How I Came to Moscow

Half awake, I imagined myself still at Surazhy and tried to remember how many days were left till Easter when a cool breeze caressed my face. The *kibitka*'s hood had been taken off while I slept, and now I opened my eyes to the immensity of an unclouded sky. "Why, I am free, free," I realized, and such a joy filled my heart that I sat up and broke into a song. It was good to be free and be able to sing after that long, dumb winter.

I finished. Somewhere behind, Kolubin's voice roared: "What did I tell you, Timoshka? Sings like a nightingale! No wonder those pious scoundrels clung to him like leeches! Why, he would have made their choir famous all over the country.

"But they never knew I could sing, sir," I shouted back and jumped down to the ground.

We had stopped on the flat bank of a narrow river, the slate-gray waters flecked gold by the sun. Three piebald horses were peacefully grazing close by. On the opposite bank, a few mild-faced cows were staring at us. Not a chimney, not a spire to be seen anywhere. The little river, the fields, and a distant wood—there seemed nothing else in the world, and I breathed freely and hungrily.

"Good health, lad," boomed Kolubin, "and here is my Timoshka, the greatest treasure ever born of a woman, I reckon."

Timoshka laughed. Small, plump, his shabby dark green *poddevka* belted with a length of rope for a girdle, his seamed face the color of a nut, and his gray eyes as clear as those of a boy, he looked at one with the green field, the running water, the sky, sharing their trueness to the uttermost. Meeting him increased the morning's pleasure for me.

"Surazhy is far behind you, lad," said Kolubin. "We did rest the horses once or twice, but never for long. And now we are going to have a good lazy spell. We did not wake you when we broke our fast. It's past noon now, and here is dinner. Eat for your health's good."

We fed by the very edge of the water, our bare toes dangling in it. We drank foaming golden-brown *kvass*. There was cold stuffed pike, some pickled mushrooms, and hunks of rye bread. "Lenten fare," grumbled Kolubin, and I laughed.

And so it was after those appallingly meager meals at the abbey.

Timoshka finished chewing, crossed himself, sprawled on the grass, and was snoring away in a moment. Kolubin and I carried the few crocks back to the *kibitka*. Now I could see that its spacious floor was covered with many bulging sacks.

"Did you buy it all at the abbey, sir?" I asked and he almost glared at me.

"Never a rotten carrot did I buy there, and never do I go there again, Judases every man of them! But I've paid them back nicely, haven't I?"

I thought that his laughter would wake Timoshka. But it did not. The little man, having driven all through the night, would not have been wakened by gunfire. Kolubin leaned against a back wheel and pulled out a stumpy little pipe.

"No, lad, that's the stuff I have bought elsewhere, and I am going to sell it once we get to Kaluga. And there I hope to buy something else. That is how it goes—buying and selling, selling and buying. And I deal in everything—from mushrooms and brass buttons to horses and timber." He laughed. "Even bast for sandals does not come amiss. I move from place to place, lad. I have got a small steading of my own to the north of Kiev. The wife and the boys are there, and I get there between whiles. Now we are making for Kursk—I have ten men waiting there and twenty-eight horses and nine carts all laden with good stuff for the great fair at Kaluga. That is how it goes. And from Kaluga I go down south—right across the Dnieper, lad." He stopped to puff at his pipe and gestured at the two pikes and some pistols on top of a sack in the *kibitka*. "You need not look so scared, lad. There are brigands all over the place . . ." He paused for a minute. "It is a good life, Mark. I deal fairly and I expect other folk to be just as straight with me, see what I mean?"

I nodded.

Kolubin had been open enough with me, and I thought I could do no better than pay him back in the same coin. I felt I could trust him, and it was a relief to turn my back on all fables about the farrier uncle in Moscow. The young grass felt soft and silken to the touch, the wind was a caress, and it was good to know myself free once again. So words came easily—about my strange discovery that I could sing, my hunger to learn "all about it," my father's views about the future, and my resolve to get to St. Petersburg and to see the Hetman.

"You carry enough powder for ten muskets, lad," Kolubin said slowly when I had done. "As soon as I saw you, I knew you were not made of cream cheese. But how in the world do you think you would get near the Hetman? St. Petersburg is not Kaluga, and he is the most important man in the capital, so folks tell me."

"I have heard that he is very kind to his countrymen," I said stubbornly. "Someone from Moscow said the Hetman likes repeating: 'We are all *khokhli* together.' "

"Still," remarked Kolubin, "he is the Hetman and a count. However, I wish you luck."

It proved a long enough trek, and we made many halts. There was a place somewhere near Kursk with a fair going on. We stopped for quite a few hours there, and I left the *kibitka* and plunged into the crowd, with Timoshka beside me. Suddenly he tugged at my sleeve. "Give them a little song, boy. They'll like it. Singing, laughing, and dancing are the best wares at any fair."

I knew he was right, but I hesitated for a moment. Then I began a short song about the harebell and the bee. People certainly liked it. The few who were the first to stop and stare soon became a sizable crowd. At the end, I had a handful of coppers, and I somersaulted for pleasure.

"Now I can do something for him," I cried to Timoshka, who stared at me.

"Mean you want to give the brass to the master? He'll knock you down if you dare."

"But—but—" I stammered, "all the food and, and—"

Timoshka spat furiously.

"What's a herring here and there got to do with it?" he shouted at me. "Take him for an innkeeper, do you? That is not the way the master looks at friendship, lad."

"I only meant—" I began, crimson to the tip of my ears, and Timoshka's anger vanished like a thin pencil of smoke.

"I know what you meant," he said, clapping me on the shoulder, "and it does you honor. But you should keep the brass, lad. If I were you, I'd try to get a bit more."

At Kursk we were joined by Koluba's train—ten men, twenty-eight horses, and nine cumbrous carts heavily laden with all the stuff he meant to sell at the great fair in Kaluga. I felt shy of the men—all of them Russians, whose speech was not always easy to follow, and it comforted me to be driving in the *kibitka* because Timoshka was no longer a stranger.

Past Livny on the Sossna we drove through an immense deep forest. I nodded when Timoshka asked me if I could handle a pike. "Just you slash at anyone jumping from behind a tree," he muttered, and placed a big pistol across his knees, and I knew I was frightened, for the brigands were a real menace in our country at that time even as they are today. The ride was none too broad; it twisted and turned most alarmingly, but Timoshka and the others knew their way. We had to make a halt in the middle, but the horses were not loosed from the shafts and the men fed hurriedly, their weapons handy. We met no brigands, possibly because there were too many of us, but I felt happy when the great forest was left behind, and then wondered whether there were many such between Moscow and St. Petersburg.

We went on and on. At Yeletz I was in luck and added a silver coin to my small hoard. At Belev on the south bank of the Oka, the mere sight of a monk in the distance made me jump back into the *kibitka*—to Timoshka's amusement. Farther on, at Chekalin, a kindly old woman added a shirt to the copper she gave me and said I should get back home. "Surely your parents will have found a bride for you by now—unless you are an orphan."

"N-no," I replied, blushing wildly. I had forgotten all about Nastia and her jangling necklaces, but I could not very well tell a stranger that I had adventure for my bride.

About a day's drive from Kaluga we made a fairly long halt because Kolubin wanted to give the final check to his stock before getting to the fair. It was early morning, and we stopped at a glorious spot. The opposite bank of the wide Oka was girdled with limes. Our own bank was flat, the ground enameled with cowslips and buttercups, and broad swathes of loosestrife. The field just behind was thick with ripe blueberries, with purple gleams of self-heal here and there. It was good to look at.

But there was no time for idleness. Kolubin got out of the *kibitka* and gave orders to the men. One by one the carts were emptied of their burden, and presently I saw what was a market in miniature spread on the lush silken grass. Carpets, copper jugs and pans, buttons of all colors and sizes, bunches of gay ribbons, strings of glass beads—red, green, blue, and yellow—bolts of linen, crudely painted pottery, sacks of nuts and dried mushrooms, basketfuls of winter apples, skeins of red wool and of gray, undressed leather, tubs of honey, and buttons again—gold and silver, red and blue, green and yellow. All of it spread out on the grass to catch the morning sun. Indeed, it was a brave sight.

Timoshka and I soon finished emptying the *kibitka*. The other men had much to do, and Timoshka and I were told to get the dinner. Soon enough he got a fire going, hung an iron caldron over it, and threw handfuls of *grecha* into the boiling water, adding a huge chunk of pork. The gruel would be seasoned with herbs, salt, and onions. I gathered basketfuls of blueberries, and Timoshka, stirring the savory mess in the caldron, told me where to find the cheese and the *kvass*. The dinner was nearly ready, but the men had not finished. Timoshka laid the large wooden spoon on the grass and glanced toward the bank where Kolubin's goods lay spread in all their richness.

"Ah," said Timoshka, "the master is clever. If it is not one thing, it is another with him."

I heard him but I did not answer. In a flash it came to me that Kolubin was something of an artist in his own right. I could not explain it in any other way, but I know that for one short moment I envied him the life he led—full of excitement as it was.

Then the men came along and we sat down to dinner.

The weather broke the same evening, and we reached Kaluga in a deluge—mud axle-deep along the main street. We put up—with no greater comfort than could be expected—at the deacon's house, so called by mere courtesy. It was just two low-ceiled rooms below and two above, joined by the creaking apology of a ladder. Kolubin, Timoshka, and I were told we could leave our gear in a corner of the front room. The rest of Kolubin's men had to shift as best they could—the only inn in the town was overcrowded. Kaluga teemed with merchants, peddlers, gypsies, and others besides, all of them shouting and cursing at the weather since the great fair was to open in less than a week and the ground was just a vast sea of thick brown mud, it having rained steadily for several days.

However, brisk business was being done all the time, and for about three days I saw nothing of Kolubin and Timoshka except at meals. Bad weather would not have kept me indoors, but I had already seen far too many monks and other clerics in among the crowds, and I did not venture out. That barely furnished front room seemed wholly ours. Neither the deacon nor his wife ever came into it. The shriveled pasty-faced woman allowed Timoshka the use of the stove in the back room. I could hear her plaintive voice behind the thin partition. The only thing she spoke about—and that always at great length—was the bad bean harvest two years before.

Meanwhile, I decided to leave for Moscow as soon as the weather improved. There was still another matter to settle before I left. Timoshka having told me that I must not offer any money to Kolubin, I wondered what possible return there was for me to make.

The matter came to be resolved soon enough—and that in a least expected manner.

We had been in Kaluga three or four days when Kolubin asked me to help him with some accounts one morning. Timoshka had gone out, and to judge by the stillness beyond the back wall, neither the deacon nor his wife was at home. Kolubin and I settled down by the tiny window and began casting up the accounts. The sun was shining bravely, and he remarked that it looked as though some of the deep mud would seen be gone.

Then, the job done, he leaned against the wall and said in a, to him, strangely quiet voice: "Mark, it is well nigh on two months that you have been with me. Now I know you've a head on your shoulders. You are good at figures and you have a way of your own with people. I reckon you could sell them next year's snow, and you and my dear Timoshka have got on famously."

He paused to pull at his pipe and I said: "And who wouldn't, sir? Timoshka is one of God's good men. And you—you—" I faltered, and he made a dismissing gesture.

"You have roving blood in you, lad. You would never have settled down at Bielogorka. As you told me, there will be your sister's husband to see to things, and your father must have washed his hands of you by now."

Again Kolubin stopped. Now I saw his drift and my heart began beating wildly.

"You have told me what you wish to do, and you have no end of pluck, lad, but pluck on its own is not a good horse to ride. I know you have a rare gift, but just think—a sharp cold in your chest, and where is the gift? No matter how fine, a voice is not a coffer of coins kept under the bed. Now the life I lead is not a swansdown mattress—what with unpaid bills and taxes and brigands on the road and all the rest of it—but I reckon it is well worth it. So will you stay with me, lad? In the end, there will be a small steading for you, a chest full of honest brass and, maybe, a wife after your own heart. What about it? See, I have taken to you from the start. Plucky and gifted you certainly are—also a bit of a fool sometimes—pinning all your faith on the Hetman, whom you are never likely to meet."

My face was crimson. My hands and knees were shaking. So was my voice: "Sir, I owe you so much. I do wish I could make you some return and prove my gratitude."

He broke in roughly: "None of that fiddle-faddle. Leave it to women, Mark. I got you away from that abbey to settle a score—and that's all there is to it. The rest isn't worth half a broken button."

I struggled on: "Sir, you have just said I was a bit of a fool. I know I am. Let me stay as I am—"

"What about thinking it over?"

I shook my head. "I could not do any other—I mean, I must make for Moscow."

Kolubin's eyes darkened. He spoke coldly: "Please yourself. There is a good enough road from here to Moscow."

"Sir," I mumbled, and he got up.

"You are old enough to be your own master."

"If you say so—"

"I have said so," he thundered, and left the room.

I saw him stalking away down the street and I knew that a curtain had fallen, and it made me miserable. I also knew that I could not face either Kolubin or Timoshka again. I can only suppose that the fool in me was uppermost that morning. I left the deacon's house within an hour, nothing clear in my mind and no food in my satchel. I went on blindly and by mere chance found myself on the main road to Moscow.

It proved the most wearying trek of all. At Ugorsk I realized how shabby I was, and parted with a few coppers for a new shirt. Between Serpukhov and Podolsk I had to tramp through a sad stretch of countryside. A long drought having killed the harvest, hunger stalked from village to village, and nobody would have welcomed any songs. There were many days when I had to ration myself. I prefer not to remember them.

The Sparrow Hills were carpeted yellow, red, and bronze by the time I saw the white walls of Moscow below.

9

The Wonder of Moscow

Since running away from Bielogorka, I had passed through a
number of towns, beginning with Mirgorod, none very beautiful and all stamped with squalor, but their traffic, crowds,
shops, and the general pace of life had left me speechless with
amazement. Yet none of it had prepared me for what I found
in the ancient capital of Russia, washed by three rivers,
girdled by the white walls of the Kremlin, and the dull red
walls of the China Town, curiously onion-shaped blue and
gilded cupolas, slated roofs and glazed windows, wide streets
and narrow lanes, echoes of bells everywhere and shouts of
peddlers at every corner, and crowds milling up and down,
buying, selling, loitering, laughing, shouting, and even dancing. . . . Having as yet not seen any sea, I could not then
imagine myself a minnow lost in its depths, but some such
comparison does come into mind today.

It was a crystal-clear, warm autumn morning. I knew I
must find some shelter for the night, but the day was still
young. I wandered on until I reached the fringe of an
enormous marketplace and remembered that I had had no

breakfast. One of my jealously hoarded copper coins got me a mug of milk and a couple of lavishly buttered *kalachi*. The burly, bearded man behind the stall laughed at my accent.

"First day in Moscow?" he asked. "Well, *khokhol*, God stay with you."

I thanked him and moved away. I saw that in between the rows of roughly timbered stalls clusters of people stood watching wrestlers, acrobats, jugglers. A tattered girl, her voice as thin as a cotton thread, was working her slow way through a very mournful song, and a gypsy woman, her red-shawled head bent low, was telling someone's fortune. In Moscow more than elsewhere, crowds seemed hungry for entertainment, but for the first time in my life I felt numb and vaguely anxious. Crowds had never frightened me before, but here I knew myself to be an intruder, and I hurried away from that large square.

I believe I wandered about for the rest of that day. I passed a few inns where well-moneyed folk could find food and refuge. I noticed that every church porch—and they could not be counted—was thick with beggars. I did not consider myself a beggar and I had not enough funds for an inn.

At last, almost at the close of the afternoon, I found myself in a maze of twisting alleys, their humpy wooden houses looking so frail that a gale would have brought them down. I rounded a corner and a burly man in a long green coat and very dirty boots all but knocked me down. He stopped, swaying a little, his small red-lidded eyes anything but friendly.

I scooped up enough courage to ask: "Please, master, where could I find a bite and a bed?"

"You—a vagrant," he asserted thickly. "Go back where you belong, *khokhol*—more than enough of your kind here."

Fury welled up in me.

"And you—you—" I spluttered, "are a *Moskal* and no Christian."

I quite thought he would hit me. I was no match for him but I certainly meant to hit back. Instead he stood, arms akimbo, and laughed till tears began rolling down his fat cheeks.

"Good stuff in you, lad, eh? I meant no harm, and what

should I be but a *Moskal*, seeing I was born and bred here, you tell me that! Well, lad, seeing what you are like, I would bed and board you but I dare not—the wife's mother lives with us and she is the kind who would grudge a spider his fly, see? But you go straight on, turn left and then right, and you come to St. Barbara's-on-Hens'-Legs. Not much of a market but the folks there are kindly." Again he laughed. "Many a time they sheltered me when the wife's mother got too bad for an angel to endure her. Now remember—straight on, left, right—St. Barbara's."

I thanked him and moved off. Here, I said to myself, was Moscow's first gift to me: St. Barbara's-on-Hens'-Legs. The name of the place where my mythical uncle was supposed to live was St. Barbara's. The name stood for a happy omen, and hunger forgotten, I trudged on.

It proved a hemmed-in place, and I could not tell which of its four churches—one to each corner—was St. Barbara's. The place was hedged about with roughly timbered cottages, and a row of ramshackle stalls stretched down its length. The late afternoon sun gilded all the spoons, nails, bits of second-hand harness, bast sandals, and what food such an obviously poor neighborhood came to buy. At the very first stall a gray-haired woman, her voluminous blue apron answering both for bodice and kirtle, sat behind a tub of pickled apples, some wooden spoons and tarnished brass buttons, a few pasties and a mound of flat rye cakes. Rather unwilling to let my speech betray me, I pointed at one of the pasties. When she answered me, I all but upset her tub of apples by flinging my arms around her neck—so lovely was it to hear the Ukrainian accent in that alien city. I spoke in our common language, and she scrambled up to her feet, wept, and crossed herself.

"Ah, but that is as good as a red egg on Easter Day."

She drew me behind her stall. There, seated on an up-turned barrel, I feasted on four cabbage-and-meat pasties and some apples, and drank water out of a dented tin mug. When I offered her money, she lightly struck at my hand.

"Take me for a heathen, do you? Now then, any kin of yours here? Where will you lie tonight, lad?"

"Oh, anywhere." I tried to speak casually. "Nights are not very cold yet, and I have got my sheepskins."

"And you won't have them, come dawn," she said grimly. "As soon as dark falls, all decent folk are indoors here— nowhere else is it safe—all the thieves and cutthroats roaming about—except under church porches, and how could you spend a night there among the beggar folk?"

"Oh, I'll manage."

"Yes, you will—by coming to me. Time I left here! Just help me shift my gear, will you?"

She lived quite close, in Bogodanny Pereulok, behind one of the churches, and certainly the name answered: God-given Lane. Aunt Lusha, once of Perozhy, near Kiev, could not have lived anywhere else, herself God's true gift to me. Generous as only the real poor can be generous, unbeaten by trouble and grief—she had lost her husband and three sons in the Persian wars—the little woman went from one day to another as though all of them were gaily flowered fields.

Her timbered shack was just one fairly spacious room, but the tiled roof was sound and the single glazed window had a stout shutter to it. A large stove, some bedding in a corner, a shelf for pots and pans, a table and a trestle—there were no other furnishings, but to me it seemed a palace. The com- bined aromas of sharp pickles, herring, linseed oil, leather, and fresh bread were sweeter than incense.

Aunt Lusha saw that I was spent. She arranged a pallet in a corner, got supper ready, and asked no questions. The food eaten, I threw myself down on the straw and slept dreamlessly until she woke me.

"I am off to the market, lad," she said, smiling, "and you stay here at ease. There is water by the stove and some food on the table."

The milk, the rye bread and bacon tasted good. I ate my fill, tidied the crocks away, and fell asleep again.

I woke when the afternoon was slipping away and the late sun was streaking the pale walls with gold and crimson, and I lay very still. I was in Moscow, one more lap ahead of me before I reached the north—and then? Disaster or not? I did not greatly care. I felt too happy for any misgivings to steal into my thoughts.

Presently Aunt Lusha was back. She bade me a cheerful good evening, lit a tallow candle, and began getting a meal. I was hungry, the onion stew and a luscious golden-brown carrot pie looked tempting, but I shook my head.

"I can't eat unless you let me pay for it."

"Give me some brass, then, proud young cockerel that you are," Aunt Lusha retorted almost crossly.

But the next moment she was laughing.

We had eaten. I pushed the trestle nearer the stove. Suddenly the room fell very still, and I knew that I owed her more than money.

"I come from Bielogorka, near Malinovy," I began.

Aunt Lusha propped her chin with one roughened brown hand and listened without interrupting once, and I knew it was good to have her as a listener. I gave her the entire story—with two gaps only. Not a word did I say about Surazhy, and because of the omission, it seemed impossible to mention that I knew my letters: the Bielogorka background would rather have quarreled with that accomplishment.

I finished. She never moved. Nor did she hurry to make her comment. When she gave it, some of it seemed surprising.

"A voice is God's gift, lad," she began, "and it is wicked to

119

bury such gifts. But there are many ways of crossing a field, and you should have chosen a better way. However hard and unloving your parents were, the manner of your leaving them does not smell good to me, lad, and you have done nothing to make it any sweeter since you left. Surely that man you fell in with knew his letters. Oh, lad, you should have asked him to write a long letter for you and explain things and ask your parents' pardon." She shook her kerchiefed head once or twice. "There is much fire in you—but you don't always remember that a fire should be damped down to make it last. Otherwise . . . ah, Queen of Heaven, it is hard when there is nothing but cold ashes in the heart, my little pigeon."

"But they never cared," I mumbled. "My father despised me. And my mother—never once did she kiss me."

"Love does not breathe by fondling only," Aunt Lusha remarked dryly and shook her head again.

Then she became practical. She knew a parish clerk in the neighborhood and a letter to Bielogorka must be written without delay. Again there was no question of my leaving Moscow before spring: frosts came early enough in the north and I would be tempting Providence if I ventured on such a long tramp before Easter at the earliest. There was a very good road and Aunt Lusha added that she would contrive to send a message to a kinswoman of hers married to a baker at Tver—midway between Moscow and St. Petersburg.

"And she will settle things for you from there on, Mark. Yes, I have heard folk say the Hetman is a kind man, and God grant you may meet him once you get there."

"Stay in Moscow till the spring?" I faltered. "But where?"

"Here, of course," Aunt Lusha retorted, and her voice

silenced me. After a pause, she spoke wistfully: "And what wouldn't I give to hear "Marussenka" again. Happen you know it, lad?"

For reply I sang the old song.

When I finished, Aunt Lusha stayed quiet. She neither smiled nor cried. She merely said, "Yours is a honey voice, lad. Now do you think you could sing at a merchant's wedding? Father Vassily of St. Nicholas'-on-the-Bear-Stump could arrange it."

"Oh, rather," I said fervently.

"That," said Aunt Lusha, "might put a few more coppers into your pouch, lad. You will need the money up there in the north. I have heard folk say that prices are shocking in St. Petersburg, and what wonder—in an alien city—for all it is the capital today."

Father Vassily arranged it, and I went to sing at the merchant's wedding. I did not really like it. The house was big, airless, and crowded, and most of the guests were drunk by the time I got there. I knew that nobody listened to my singing, but the merchant pushed a big silver coin into my hand when I had finished and he said that everybody was pleased. Then he shouted to one of the servants to take me to the kitchen. Standing in a corner, I nibbled at a piece of hare pie, and ran away as soon as I could, nobody remarking on my going.

"Now, lad, what is amiss?" Aunt Lusha wanted to know.

I said angrily, "I sang, I gave them of my best, and they treated me as though I were a scullion—grubbing away in the pantry. . . ."

Aunt Lusha pushed the trestle toward the wall, sat down,

and looked at me as though she were seeing me for the first time. I felt uncomfortable.

"Come spring, will you go back to Bielogorka?" she asked at last.

I stared at her. "Go back? Why, Aunt Lusha, I am nearly where I had wanted to get to—"

"No. You are at the very beginning, lad." She paused and began kneading her kirtle. "And were you treated any better at Mirgorod?"

"They cheated me there. It is quite different here. I had a silver ruble given me."

"Well, did you expect a seat next to the bridegroom, and to have wine served to you in a silver cup? Now take that scowl off your face, lad, and listen to me. God willing, you may reach the end of your road one day, but the gift you've got means service first and last. Yes, you serve folks when you sing to them—whether they pay you or not. What does it matter if they treat you as a servant? They have paid you handsomely, and that is the end of it, but many hard kicks will come your way unless you learn to bridle your temper." She rose and moved toward the stove. "Now it is time we had our supper."

Aunt Lusha did not cure my hasty temper but she had no further occasion to break into a homily. Never again did I come back, my face as sour as a lemon. Such depths of shame had she stirred in me that evening that I felt I owed it to her to rein in my fury when, as happened all too often, a coin would be thrown to me and I had to pick it up off the floor, or when the mistress of the house or even her cook would order me to stop in the middle of a song because the master and his guests had fallen asleep and "the noise" might waken them.

No, I did not take to the Muscovites. They were generous, gay, and hospitable to a fault. They were also incredibly dirty and coarse. I had seen some hard-drinking in Ukraina. Here they did not just drink: they soaked themselves. And the lawlessness appalled me. Crime of every color stalked the streets by night and even by day. In my dim untutored way I imagined all of it was due to some people having far too much money to spend, though, on the other hand, I had never seen such stark penury. Beggars were as plentiful as bilberries in June and they crowded practically every street. My first wanderings over, I took to spending my leisure indoors, carving spoons for Aunt Lusha's little stall, keeping the place tidy, and even learning to cook. Whatever I thought of the city, her tiny home still remained a palace, and she its true heartbeat.

I was sad to leave her, but the first shy signs of spring were heartening to watch. Aunt Lusha had already sent a message to the baker's wife at Tver. At last came the morning when, my satchel filled with good things for the journey, we both halted by the door. I felt tongue-tied, tears brimming in my eyes. She, crying a little, made the sign of the cross over my forehead and did not say much. There was no need for many words between us. I now believe that Aunt Lusha was the very first person to teach me that nobody should wholly belong to themselves, that any gift is a responsibility, and that, finally, in her own words: "Life would be easier for most folk if they did not forget God's sunlight in the November dark."

10

When Danger Overtook Me . . .

I had felt so walled-in during my months in Moscow that it was a relief to find myself on the road again. Certainly, it was a good road to walk, and the spring having burst in, everything I saw offered delight, the swift clear streams, robins and thrushes perched on greening boughs, fields fully awake from their winter sleep, stretches of common land carpeted with brave young grass. The sun warmed but did not scorch, the wind was pleasant, and even the dust raised by the passing of many wheels could be endured. I trudged on with a will. Many carriages and men on horseback passed me. Nobody took the least notice of me, and I was glad of it.

Nothing of note happened during the first three days. Then, having spent a night in a barn at a hamlet called Kurilka, I set my face to the north again. I had reached Kurilka the evening before, with a peasant wedding going on, and the bride's parents had invited me in. I had paid for food and shelter with a merry song or two, and everybody had been pleased. Now I set out, my heart light and my satchel heavy with all the good things they had crammed into it.

The sun was high when I came to a spot where a brook threaded its narrow silver way close to the edge of the road. I stopped there, washed my face and hands, and sprawled on the grass to untie the satchel thongs.

Then I heard hoofs along the road.

The sound was familiar enough and it did not startle me. But suddenly the three riders drew rein and stared at me. The horses seemed well enough but the men looked shabby, and when I saw the sun glint across the pistols stuck into their belts, I decided I did not like them at all. None the less, I replied to their stare by wishing them the time of day. I knew I was frightened and hoped that my voice did not give me away.

My greeting was not returned. They just sat their horses and went on staring. I fumbled in my satchel for an onion pie, and my heart took to thumping.

Then one of the riders, a portly, middle-aged man with a great scar on his right cheek and strangely hooded eyes, called out hoarsely, "Eh, and who may you be, young gentleman?"

The two younger men roared with laughter.

"Need you ask, Golub? His voice is enough—a count's runaway son from Ukraina, most likely."

I tried to steady my hands, but they kept shaking. "Is it any concern of yours who I am?"

The man with the scar shook his head. "Well, these are unquiet times—many wicked folk prowl about. Not good to be on your own. You making for Tver, eh?"

I did not answer.

"Well, what about us keeping you company? We are bound for Tver, young gentleman."

"You are mounted, and I am on foot."

He laughed. "Ah, but that can be put right in a trice."

Before I realized what was happening, the man jumped out of the saddle and picked me up as though I were a feather-stuffed doll. I opened my mouth to scream and he clamped a rough, sweaty hand against my mouth. I tried to struggle free, but his grip was like iron. Within a few instants he was back in the saddle. The three horses were turned off the road into the field and made to gallop toward a wood in the distance. I heard the man mutter, "Steady, now, young master, steady now . . . All for your own good."

I gave up struggling. He took his hand off my mouth and I no longer wanted to scream because it seemed useless—there was not a soul in sight. We reached the wood and plunged into it. I closed my eyes. Presently I knew the man was

reining in. I heard raucous laughter behind me and wondered if they were going to kill me there on the spot.

They did not. The man who had captured me sprang out of the saddle, still holding me in his arms. Then he pushed me into a dirty, smoky hut all but hidden among the elms and birches. I staggered in, dimly conscious of several packages lying on the earthen floor, bits of harness and barrels of beer. There was no furniture. There were no windows. There would have been no air if the little door were not kept open, but one of the younger brigands straddled across the threshold. In any case, dazed and scared though I was, I realized that an attempt to run away was hopeless.

Golub and the other man began stripping me. Aunt Lusha

127

had cared for my scant wardrobe. Some of the money earned at weddings and christenings had laid out in a brief blue coat and two shirts. Well, they took all the clothes I had on, including the belt, ripped it open, found the gold piece, and the rest of my hoard, and whistled.

"H—m, Semka," muttered Golub, "maybe you were right! I thought he looked like a young gentleman. . . ."

There was nothing I could do or say. They emptied the satchel and what clean underwear there was went to join the rest of my things, and my small hoard of coins as well. Semka grinned and flung a worn-out gray shirt and a pair of patched blue breeches at me.

"Leave the sandals be," mumbled Golub. "They would not fetch half a copper." He seated himself on the floor, his enormous hairy hands clasping his knees, and stared at me very hard.

"What have you got to say?" he asked gruffly.

Tears I would not shed were nearly choking me. I clenched my fists very hard. In a broken voice I told them that I had nothing else in the world and would they please let me go?

The walls of the hut all but shook at their guffaws. Did I think it was all a joke, they wanted to know. Let me go so that I could raise the alarm at the very next village? Did I imagine they were born the day before yesterday?

"I promise not to tell anyone," I said faintly.

Behind me, from the doorway, came a sneering voice: "What are you wasting time for, mates? Take him to the first oak we see and put an end to it."

Golub snarled. "What—all for some clothes and one gold coin? No, Pavlik—" and he turned to me. "Which part of Ukraina do you come from? And mind, tell us the truth."

Then I understood. They were after ransom. Shaking and stammering, I came out with a number of fictitious details, settling Bielogorka—under a different name—close to Zaporozhy—three days' hard ride from my home, enlarging my father's estate and his status in the neighborhood, and giving my late godfather's surname as my own. They listened and asked no questions. Then Semka, who must have come from a different social level than the other two, got up and fumbled in a pile of rubbish in a corner. He turned around, a sheet of thick gray paper in his hand, and ordered me to say it all over again. I watched his hand move up and down the paper.

When the last word had been put down, he muttered to Golub: "What do you say? One hundred rubles or two—perhaps more?"

"That'll be for Tikh to settle once we've got the lad off our hands."

"When?"

"Just before dawn, I reckon."

"Risky," grumbled Semka. "Such a lot of traffic around about Luky."

"We'll clear that spot before dawn. Nobody travels this road by night."

Pavlik laughed unpleasantly. Some folks did, he said, and it was so much the better for *them*.

Then Golub turned to me and made a speech. "Listen, Timofey Bobyla," he began. "No harm will come to you if you behave properly and if your parents realize that we mean business. We are poor men and have to earn our living, so if your father does not agree, it is your head that will be sent to Ukraina. Is that clear?"

"Y-yes," I stammered in a voice which did not belong to me.

Then they fell upon the food they had found in my satchel. When they had finished, Golub tossed a piece of bacon and some bread at me. I could not eat and asked for water.

I think it was the worst day in my life. Time dragged on leaden feet. When night came, I could not sleep. It was still dark when the ruffians began getting ready for the road, and I was warned by Golub that his pistol was loaded and that he would put a bullet through me if I dared raise any alarm. I heard it almost indifferently. The disaster and the wakeful night seemed to have robbed me of all my wits. I was almost past caring whether they killed me or not.

The sweet pure air of the wood helped to revive me. The brigands must have overslept, because dawn was just about to break when we reached the open road. I could smell the dew on the grass and hear the first songs of birds, and though I was held in Golub's iron grip, a faint hope began stirring in me. It was rather foolish since at that time there was nothing for me to hope for.

We were galloping along the road edged with aspens on one side. Quite suddenly a mist came down, and the three men had to slacken their pace.

"Bad luck," muttered Semka. "We'll miss that turn as likely as not—and there is a deep ditch behind the trees, too—no good leaving the road."

The mist thickened. Golub swore and veered his horse toward the trees.

"Better wait a spell, mates—we are not far from the turn."

I cannot now remember how long we waited under those trees, but presently the mist began lifting in patches.

"Well, mates," said Golub, "we'd better be off." He began

turning his horse back to the road when we heard the rumble of wheels somewhere behind. I saw Semka's hand fly to the pistol tucked into the belt. I saw Pavlik lick his lips. I heard Golub murmur: "Never an ill wind, brothers," and he tightened his arm around my waist and hissed: "One sound from you, youngster, and it is all up with you."

Semka and Pavlik jumped from their saddles and pulled me down. One of them pushed me toward the nearest tree and tied me to it. Then they remounted. The rumble grew more and more distinct. I peered—and out of the patchy mistiness I saw a huge *rydvan* lumber toward us. It was painted a bright yellow and was drawn by six horses.

The brigands veered to the right. Sharp as a pebble came a shout from Golub: "Halt and deliver!"

The horses halted at once. I saw the ashen faces of coachman and postilion. I saw Pavlik's horse move forward and I saw his arm upraised, and I shook like an aspen leaf.

What happened the very next moment came with the swiftness of lightning. Three shots rang from the lowered window of the *rydvan*. The first bullet missed and hit a tree quite close to me. The other two went home. Pavlik and Golub, both unsaddled, rolled to the ground, and their horses at once galloped away. Next, Semka aimed, but the bullet ricocheted off the roof of the coach. Before he had time to aim again, the fourth bullet from the *rydvan* went home, and he fell from the saddle and lay still. One could hardly have called it a battle: it was just a shambles.

Terror-struck, I stared. The three men lay very still where they had fallen, the young grass dyed deep crimson all around them. The coachman and the postilion were doing their

131

upmost to quiet the six horses. Then the door of the *rydvan* opened and three men in elegant traveling clothes came out very leisurely, the youngest of them saying: "It is a good morning's work, to account for three highwaymen."

"Yes, and we had better report it at Tver."

Then they saw me. They stared and exchanged remarks I could not hear. I saw them fingering their gleaming pistols and I mustered what shreds of strength I had to scream: "I

was not with them. They caught me. They tied me to this tree."

I saw them exchange glances. I heard one of them say, "Take care, Nicholas, it may well be a trap," and then my knees gave, my head sank to my chest, and I saw and heard no more.

When I came around, we were on the road. So luxurious was the yellow velvet upholstery of the coach and so elegant were the clothes of the three gentlemen that I grew most painfully conscious of my own filthy tattered garments.

The three men waited a little. Then the eldest of them said quite kindly, "Take a sip, boy. That will put you right."

I pressed my lips against the silver rim of a flask. The brandy ran like fire down my throat. I shook my head when he wanted me to drink again. I leaned back and stared at my companions. I wished I could thank them, but my voice seemed to have gone and my hands were still shaking. Never had I felt so ill at ease. Those three men had virtually saved my life and, however benumbed my senses, I realized it. But they came from a world I had never known, a world of large towns, pleasant smells, lace foaming at throat and wrists, snuff taken out of jeweled boxes. Their speech ran like smooth silk. When they addressed one another, their voices were subdued, almost languid. It was hard to believe that but a short while ago those white, cared-for hands had held pistols and killed three men.

They never hustled me, but, of course, they wanted to know my story. I stammered it out as best I could.

"But you are not a real beggar," murmured the eldest of the three, and I saw him glance at my patched-up breeches.

The blood rushed into my face. In a flash I remembered my gold piece and the small hoard of silver and copper coins pocketed by Golub. Whoever came to bury those bodies would find the money. . . . Well, I was a beggar indeed!

"We are stopping at Tver for a few hours," the gentleman went on. "They will want to hear all about it from you."

"No, no, please . . . Those three . . . they were members of a gang." I knit my eyebrows in the effort of remembering a casually heard name. "Their chief is called Tikh . . .

and I gave them a paper . . . I mean, it might go ill with my folk if—if—"

"I see," said the elderly gentleman. "Well, boy, have it your own way. Where were you making for when they caught you?"

"Tver, sir." That was an easy question to answer. "I—I have friends there."

They asked no further questions. In fact, they left me alone, and before the sun set, we reached Tver. It looked an enormous city to me but they referred to it as "that dirty village." I thanked them for their kindness and jumped out of the *rydvan* as soon as it stopped by the posting station. I was never to meet any of them again and I never knew their names.

Enormous as Tver seemed to me, it proved fairly easy to find the bakery tucked away at one end of a mean narrow street. Aunt Lusha's cousin I was not to meet—she happened to be away, nursing a sick relation in some village west of the town. But her husband was there, and he knew all about the message. He was a hunchback, with a very tired face and the kindest eyes I had ever seen in a man. I could see how poor the couple were, and I controlled myself enough not to tell him that I had been robbed on the way. He seemed rather astonished when I turned up—it was obvious that he had not expected a beggar. But he said nothing and began bustling about to get some sort of a meal.

When we had eaten, he said quietly: "Well, Mark, you are in clover—my nephew is leaving for St. Petersburg tomorrow with some raw hides for an English merchant there, and there will be room in the wagon for you."

I stammered, my head bent: "I—I—have no money to pay

him—" and here all self-control left me. I sobbed, pillowing my head in my arms, and told him what had happened. Presently his rough hand began stroking my raveled hair.

"Hush, lad, hush. . . . These things will happen. Ah—but Ivan will take you for Christ's sake—never you worry."

I raised my head, snatched at that roughened hand, and kissed it fervently.

11

And Not a Door Was Opened
to Me . . .

I can only suppose that searing experience on the road had
left a deeper imprint than I had imagined at the time.
However it was, the journey from Tver to the northern
capital is nothing but a blur in my memory. I remember that
Kozukh, the baker, being a poor man, could give me neither
money nor clothes—but he gave me a satchel and filled it
with what food he could spare. I remember that his nephew,
Ivan, spoke hardly at all during the whole of the three days,
but that I felt heartened by his smile. I don't know where we
stopped for meals or for the night. I suppose Ivan paid for
what shelter we got. But all of it is a blur—until we reached
the Moscow Gate in St. Petersburg and I jumped off the
wagon, thanked Kozukh's nephew, and moved away.

I knew I looked like a beggar and I was a beggar. I possessed nothing in the world except the tattered clothes I stood
up in and a hunk of rye bread together with a small piece of
bacon in the old satchel the baker had given me, but I was not
thinking of such things. I struck ahead, my head high,
walking along the cobbled roadway as though it were carpeted

with red velvet. I had got there, the sun was glorious over-head, and nothing else mattered.

That rose-colored mood did not last long. For one thing, the sun crept behind one cloud and then another, and the city took on a strangely remote gray air. For another, nobody had ever told me that St. Petersburg was built on nineteen islands, that bridges were few, and that one had to pay toll for crossing some of them. Again I was amazed to see all but tumbledown wooden cottages side by side with magnificent mansions of gray stone and of red. There were hardly any beggars to be seen and far fewer churches than in any town I had been through. But what struck me most was the sharply alien feel of the capital. I had tramped through most of Ukraina and right across central Russia. St. Petersburg, I sensed, belonged to neither. It was itself—but the self it had was hard to understand. People hurried so, and they wore an absorbed, indifferent look. I wandered on and on, my heart sinking. I just knew I would never be able to stand at a corner of any market square in that strange and lovely city and sing to please its people.

And then I said to myself that I was a fool, shook the doubt and anxiety out of my mind, and went on and on until I reached the banks of the Neva. There I gaped and gasped and gazed. Here was a queenly sister to my own dear Dnieper, I thought, looking at the deep blue river almost hungrily. I had not a coin for toll bridges, ferries, or boats—but had I not swum from boyhood?

Suddenly I heard voices behind me and turned to see a ramshackle two-wheeled cab pull up. An enormously fat woman in a dark green cloak got out, paid the driver, and he

138

jumped off the box and began getting her gear out of the
cab.

"I'll whistle for a boat, lady."

She nodded and took to counting her valises.

"Oh dear, I never sent word I was coming back today—and
what shall I do with all my stuff on the other bank?"

The cabman winked at me.

"Why, here is a young porter for you, lady—he'll carry
everything, won't you, lad?"

I nodded.

The woman's glance said plainly that she doubted if she
could trust me, but the little rowing boat had already drawn
alongside, and there happened to be nobody else. I picked up
three of the valises and jumped into the boat, then returned
for the other two. The boatman, I saw, looked rather as if he
wondered whether the woman would upset the boat getting
on board. Indeed, it rocked most perilously until she arranged
herself amidships.

She had not said a single word to me, and I was glad to
keep silent. It was pure heaven to be on the water, and we
crossed all too quickly as I thought. The fat woman must have
paid my fare because the boatman did not grumble, but I did
not think it was part of my duty to thank her.

By dint of roping two of the valises together and carrying
them on my back, I managed to handle the rest well enough.
The woman's house was happily quite close to the riverbank—a severe, alien-looking house of some pale stone, all its
small windows closed and curtained. Without looking at me,
the woman ordered me to put her things down by the door,
and for a moment I feared that my service would have no

other payment than the boat fare. But she loosened her purse strings and pushed two very small copper coins into my sweaty hand. Heartened by the prospect of a meal, I asked where I might find a place to eat.

Her lard-embedded eyes mocked at me, but she told me how to reach the nearest market, adding: "Mind you pay for what you get. We have enough poor folk of our own without beggars straying in from Ukraina, and you might do worse than learn to speak Russian properly, *khokhol*—"

It meant a hard effort to rein in my anger. I turned away just as the door was opening and heard her say to someone that she had forgotten to let them know of her arrival but a *khokhol* vagrant had helped her with the luggage. "A cowman's son, by the looks of him—"

I ran off, my fists clenched hard.

The market was easy enough to find, and there were many food stalls, but my heart sank when I realized how steep were the prices in the northern capital. Anywhere else, those two coppers would have assured my dinner and supper together. In St. Petersburg, a mug of thin milk, a small sausage, and an equally modest, oddly shaped loaf emptied my exchequer. I ate unhurriedly, standing by the stall, and I noticed that the woman kept a sharp eye on the mug and all but snatched it out of my hand the moment I finished the milk. I could not really blame her: I looked a vagrant, I was a beggar, and all beggars were considered thieves in those days.

I had always liked marketplaces for their movement, the excited people, the thousand and one things on the stalls, and, finally, for the chance of slipping into a corner there to clear my throat, so raise my head, and to begin singing. But that first morning in St. Petersburg I had all but forgotten the heart and core of my great ambition. I still hoped—but my hopes were flattened and colorless. All I knew was that I could never seek out the Hetman until I had put some decent clothes on my back. Meanwhile, what? I did not know.

I edged my way through the crowd and reached a narrow lane running down to a small river. The lane curved in several places and from around a corner I heard a child screaming. I rushed ahead.

There stood a portly, red-faced man in a short white coat and green breeches. With his left hand he held a tattered little boy by the scruff of his neck. With his right hand he was showering blows on the child's head, face, neck, and shoulders. Two lemons lay on the ground at the man's feet.

The man was so big, the child so small . . . The blood rushed into my face. I ran up and hit the man across the face. He staggered and loosed his hold on the child, who stopped screaming and ran away. The man roared: "From the madhouse, are you?"

So possessed by fury was he that the blow he dealt me did not hurt at all. I hit him again. But I could not match my strength against his. Within a moment or two the man had me on the ground.

"Is that enough for you, young cockerel? But wait! Now I'll give you in charge for assault. A good flogging—that is what you need."

I raised myself up and panted, "You—you—you were hitting a mere child."

"A *khokhol*, are you?" he snarled. "Well, so was my late wife, God rest her soul! They are all mad in Ukraina. Who are you to meddle? I was chastising a thief, if you want to know. He pinched these lemons out of my pocket."

"You have got them back."

"And would I have got them back if I had not caught the boy?" The man stooped for the lemons, put them into his pocket, and then stared at me. "That ends the matter, *khokhol*. Not a liver-hearted lad, are you?" He measured me with a slow glance. "Things not going well down your street, are they? Out of work, I suppose?"

I was not sure that I liked him, but here was a straw, and I clutched at it by admitting that I was looking for work.

"Any kin of yours in the city?"

I shook my head.

"Your name?"

"Mark Poltoratzky."

He blinked.

"Saints in heaven, what a mouthful! I am Ivan Dolin, a respectable clerk at the docks. Can you cook? Mine left me yesterday—the wages they expect these days—enough to ruin even the Tsarina!"

Could I cook? I thought swiftly while Dolin, arms akimbo, went on bewailing the iniquities of servants and the rising prices. I had often enough watched Gapka at Bielogorka and also helped her by plucking poultry and chopping pork and mutton for pies. I had also contrived to have supper ready for Aunt Lusha and she would eat whatever there was and not complain. I had grilled roots, mushrooms, and fish on a fire lit in the open. Was it not enough? Dolin paused to draw a breath, and I made my decision.

"I've done some cooking," I told him, "and I'll try my best."

He mentioned a wage almost casually and looked relieved when I accepted it. It must have been far less than he would have had to pay anyone else, but his offer was something of a miracle to me, and one did not argue about miracles. I meant to stay with him until I had saved enough to buy a decent coat, shoes, and breeches. I looked no further than that. I shuddered at the thought of wearing my tatters in the Hetman's presence. It seems foolish today, but I suppose I must have inherited a touch of my father's vanity.

I thanked Dolin as we made for his little house, but I said nothing about the miracle. Nor did I ever tell him about my secret ambition. I dare say it might have meant nothing to him, but I took no risks, and it was a relief to find him lacking in curiosity except where his victuals were concerned.

I never discovered what the man's office duties were. His hours were certainly odd. He would be out in the morning, return at midday, sit down by the window, and await his dinner in the manner of someone attending a religious service. He seemed to approve of most things brought to the table, and he praised my ability to haggle at the market. My predecessor, Dolin declared, must have robbed him right and left. He took fully an hour over his dinner, then settled himself for a good nap, and went out again, to be back long before sunset to enjoy his supper. Very occasionally he would retail some pieces of gossip he had picked up during the day, but such gossip would be offered with a slightly contemptuous and languid air since nothing much mattered in the world except food. Within the first few days I realized that had that poor bedraggled child stolen a handkerchief out of Dolin's pocket, the whole matter would have been settled with a cuff or two.

143

It was the theft of two lemons that had sent the man into a towering fury.

I also learned that his moods were wholly unpredictable. On some evenings he would call out to me to leave the tiny kitchen and to eat my supper at his table, but the least trifle—be it a fly drowning in his beer or a knife falling off the table—would enrage him. I would be kicked and told to make myself scarce—a hard-working man had the right to enjoy his food in peace. Again, often enough Dolin would lose his temper for no reason that anyone could see.

It did not greatly trouble me. The house was tiny and it did not take me long to tidy it in the morning. The marketing done and the two meals planned and prepared, I was at liberty to use my leisure as I thought best. So one day I found my way to Tsarina Meadow and had the Hetman's mansion pointed out to me by a kindly passer-by. It looked like a palace, with statues all along the pediment and two marble pillars supporting the porch. I stared at it, unable to imagine the splendors of the interior.

The month was gone, and Dolin handed me my wages. I laid them out in a shirt, a pair of dark blue breeches, and a pair of rather rough-looking shoes. The money went no further, but I was satisfied.

One very hot day in early June, Dolin announced that he wished for nothing but cold food for his supper, and that answered my own plans perfectly. I slipped into the closet which was allotted to me, brushed my hair tidily, put on my finery, and left the house—with Dolin still plunged into deep slumbers. I had secreted two coins from the day's marketing—I wanted to get to Tsarina Meadow by the quickest means possible and that meant hiring a boat and not crossing the river by one of the few "free" bridges.

I shall never forget the moment when, standing between those two grand marble pillars, I touched the bronze knocker. It was some time before the door was opened by an elderly man in a large green apron. He had a triangular-shaped mole on his left cheek and he gave me a look as though I were a beetle at his feet.

"How dare you knock at the front door?" he boomed, but his oddly accented Russian told me he was my countryman and I said in Ukrainian that I hoped to have the honor of speaking to the Hetman.

He laughed and pulled at his beard.

"I should have sent word to you, my young gentleman. Why, the Hetman is away—at Peterhof by the sea."

"When will he be back?"

"Never for the likes of you," he retorted and slammed the great door in my face.

Face burning, hands trembling, I went down the steps and turned toward the river. There seemed nothing left except a letter, and how was I to deliver it? If I were to hand it to the man with the mole, he would most likely tear it up as soon as my back was turned. No, I said to myself, getting into the boat which was to carry me back to all the preparations needed for the cold cucumber soup and some fish—no, a letter would never do. I must find my way into that house, and that before very long.

12

"Should I Return to Bielogorka?"

That evening my employer was in a jovial mood. He seemed pleased with life and pleased with the food I had prepared. He praised me for having spent my wages so wisely and fingered my shirt and breeches approvingly. Nor did he exile me into the kitchen when the meal was over, and I was bold enough to ask: "Where is Peterhof? Could I walk there and back in a day?"

"There and back in a day?" he echoed, frowning, and I knew I should never have taken the good mood for granted. "Rubbish! It takes hours to get there driving or riding. Go there? Is that what I pay you a good wage for?"

"I had an idea it was just one of the islands," I offered hurriedly, and Dolin snorted: "You would, *khokhol* that you are! Peterhof is not an island. It is by the sea. I have never been there. From all I have heard, it is all beaches and woods and palaces of princes and counts and suchlike. You get on with your cooking, lad, and stop talking nonsense."

I said no more. I had already made up my mind to get to Peterhof. That, of course, meant transport. I supposed farmers

146

and peddlers from St. Petersburg went down there from time to time, but in the north they would not sweep a cobweb off for you unless you paid them. So I said to myself that I must wait till the next pay day came along—nearly three weeks to wait for it—and then go, first finding out by some means or other if the Hetman was still at Peterhof.

I slipped back into the kitchen, leaving Dolin to his pipe.

It was about a week later that he came home one evening, a peculiar expression on his face. He did not stop in the front room but walked straight into the kitchen and closed the door behind him. I was so astounded that I nearly dropped the chicken pie just taken out of the oven.

"Ah, that smells good." Dolin smacked his lips. "But put it back into the oven for a minute. I have such a secret to tell you—and mind you keep it—else I'd take the stick to you." He clenched his fist. "The whole city hums with it." He paused to lower his voice: "What do you think—the Tsarina is going to be married next month—yes, at Tsarskoe, all done properly, with a Metropolitan and two archbishops, and it must all be kept a secret, seeing he is a commoner, and for another reason as well."

Evidently, he thought it a tremendous piece of news, and I tried to look as though I shared his view.

"And who is the man?"

"Why, the Hetman, who else?"

"But why should it be kept a secret?"

"Have you got hay in your head, boy? Why, he is a commoner—and she, an emperor's daughter."

"You said there was another reason?"

147

"Yes," Dolin nodded, "and a weightier one, too, at least for the people. I should say the Hetman is the most hated man in St. Petersburg."

The dishcloth I held in my hands fell to the floor. But Dolin took no notice.

"Why?" I managed to ask in a voice which did not quite belong to me.

"Too proud and rich he is, and unkind, too. Folk say he has never been known to lift his little finger for anyone."

By that time I was facing the oven and Dolin could not see the look on my face. I just managed to stutter: "I háve heard of him being kind to his countrymen."

Dolin chuckled. "Yes, to such among them whose own pockets bulge with gold and who wear diamond buckles on their shoes. You try to get as much as a broken button out of him—you'd get his door slammed in your face," and he chuckled again.

I may have eaten some supper that evening. I am not sure. I certainly did not sleep that night. I kept trying to assure myself that Dolin's stories were just stories and no more, that people in Ukraina and in Moscow could not have been wrong when they praised the Hetman for his accessibility and kindness. But it was all so difficult, and I felt as though the very last star had fallen out of my sky. I remembered the servant in that great doorway. I could still hear the slam. . . . "Like master, like servant." I wept, calling to mind the ancient saying. Could all of it be true?

Once unbosomed of "the great secret," Dolin seemed to lose all interest in it. I began listening to market chatter with far greater attention than ever before. The suggested marriage was not as much as hinted at, but all I heard about the Hetman bore out the reputation given him by Dolin. The Hetman was said to be wholly unapproachable; he had twelve noblemen for his gentlemen-in-waiting, pages served his food on bended knee, no beggar had ever been known to get any alms from him. People muttered darkly about his mansions, estates, jewels, and gold. . . . All of it I heard day by day, but a streak of stubbornness made me take refuge in reminding myself that market chatter was all too often so much spent breath. . . .

Until the day in late June when I learned that I was mistaken.

Early in the morning Dolin announced that he was going out to dinner and gave me meticulous instructions about his supper. The shopping done, I wandered off toward the river. Unaccustomed leisure hung rather heavy on my hands. I had no wish to consider food for myself, and I thought that a good stroll would do me good. My thoughts were so many tight little knots. I felt I stood at a crossroads with no signpost to guide me.

I got to the bank. It was a glorious June day, and the deep blue of the Neva was shot through with gold. An elegant barge was moored to a jetty. I stared idly. I had seen them in midstream. That one was the first I could see closely. Painted bright green and white, with deep crimson cushions amidships, six men in blue at the oars and the seventh at the tiller, it was a private craft, obviously belonging to somebody living in one of those grand stone mansions. I had never seen such elegance at close quarters. I stood, gaping. The crew took no notice of me. But suddenly the man astern raised his head, got up, and jumped on to the jetty. The rest of the men un-shipped the oars.

I turned and saw a beautiful carriage draw up. An elderly woman in a violet gown and a white bonnet alighted, followed by a young man whose lace shone like driven snow and whose brown velvet coat carried gold embroidery. I had never seen such elegance in my life. They took no notice of me. They had obviously been having an argument, and now they did not trouble to lower their voices. I heard the words "the Hetman" pronounced by the woman, and I stiffened.

"But I am telling you, Grandmama," the young man said hotly, "that it is not the slightest use. The Hetman wouldn't help his own brother out of a scrape. Don't you remember what happened when Peter Shuvalov lost all that money at cards to him? The Hetman forced him to sell an estate. . . ."

"I know, I know," interrupted the elderly lady. "All the same, I should try."

I did not see them board the elegant barge. I turned toward Dolin's house, midnight in my mind.

So the market chatter was not all spent breath. Those two, I said to myself, must have belonged to the court. They said the same thing. So it was true about the Hetman having a heart of stone. . . .

I spent that afternoon in torment. In the end I remembered there was Dolin's supper to get, but so turmoiled was my mind that I emptied the whole pepper pot into the soup, forgot the duck in the oven, put honey into the veal cutlets and salt into the raspberry pie. Dolin returned in one of his nastiest moods. He smelled the duck, tasted the soup, and cuffed me soundly. Then he turned to the cutlets. So enraged was he that he could not take good aim and the dish missed my head by a few inches. I stood and watched, unaware. My whole world having been shattered, I had no apologies to offer for the spoiled food. My wooden attitude added fuel to Dolin's wrath. He leaped from his chair, rushed into the closet, flung my new clothes on the floor, trampled on them, picked them up, and tore them to shreds. I saw it all and I did not move.

Then Dolin fell on me. For a second I thought he meant to kill me. Instead he pushed me toward the door and kicked me out.

"My wages—" I panted, "due—"

"Here are your wages," he thundered, kicked me again, and slammed the door.

For a moment or two I stood still. Through the small window left open because of the heat, I heard Dolin thumping and bumping about the room. Then I turned away—a dispossessed beggar once again, and my two years of wanderings had already taught me that no means of redress came within the reach of the very poor, still less would I have known where to go and lodge a complaint against Dolin for the withheld wages and my torn-up clothes. He owned a house, held a job, had a place in the world. I owned nothing except a tattered shirt and breeches, and a pair of bast sandals which were all but falling off my feet. Nor had I a place anywhere. Going down the little street, all sense of direction lost, I realized that nobody would have cared if I were to throw myself into one of the many rivers of the city. I also knew that I had no means of leaving St. Petersburg: one had to pay toll at every gate, and I had not a copper on me.

"But I must get back to Bielogorka somehow," I said to

myself, and for a moment the idea of seeing the Dnieper, the cherry orchards, the vast silken meadows, and silver birches around the kitchen-gardens, was almost heartening.

The next instant I halted and called myself a fool. None but a fool would try to cover those vast distances again with nothing except failure behind him. "I must not fail," I thought. "Aunt Lusha hoped I would not. My gift is still there. Something must happen, but nothing can happen if I start being sorry for myself."

Quite unaware, I reached the low bank of a river unknown to me by name. A few willows stood whispering here and there, and I saw a cluster of humpy cottages on the opposite bank. To the left of me was a small wooden church surrounded by elms and firs. There was not a soul in sight. It seemed difficult to imagine that I was still in the capital. Not a footfall to be heard anywhere, and the world was bathed in the pearly-gray light of a June night. A wind stirred the elms and refreshed my burning face. I moved toward the little church and sat down under a great tree. There I spent the brief summer night, and when I woke, I felt faint from hunger. I had foregone my dinner the day before.

Presently a tinny bell began ringing overhead. A few shabbily dressed women passed me on the way to church. One of them stopped, pity all over her wrinkled face, and stooping, put a copper into my lap.

That assured me something of a breakfast and also my fare in a ferry across the Neva. Once on the south side, I felt my spirits rising. The Summer Gardens and the Tsarina Meadow were on that island, great palaces and quite a few markets. Why, lucky chances were there for the snatching, I said to myself, and I halted on the quayside to say my prayers.

Well, I would rather not say much about the week that followed. What chances there were did not pass my way. I haunted one marketplace after another, but if anyone took notice of me it was just to shout that I should get out of the way. I saw numbers of people who sang, somersaulted, danced, and cracked jokes to amuse the crowd, and those people were given money. I dared not join them, nor could I sing on my own. It was just as though my only gift were buried somewhere deep below. I wandered about the waterfront, and not a man or woman needed my services. A few nights in the open did no good to my tatters. The shirt was dirty and torn in several places. I tried to beg and I did it so clumsily, often my voice hardly above a whisper, that nobody heard me, and I could not stretch out my hand. I spent a whole day near the Moscow Gate in the hope that at least some farmer going south would allow me to ride in his cart. My reward was a few cuffs and a threat of a whip. I must have looked even too disreputable for a casual beggar. Three times only during that week did I get any alms, and my chief means of sustenance were decayed cabbage leaves and rotten fruit picked up in marketplaces after their business was finished.

Then one morning a man asked me to carry a sack for him. I was so gnawed by hunger that even a short distance left me spent and panting. I dropped the sack so clumsily by his door that the rope snapped and some of the contents were spilled on the pavement. The man was so angry that I did not receive a tip. But in the same street I saw a baker's cart stop outside a house, and the baker, a basket on his arm, vanished through the open door. I mustered all my strength, ran up, snatched at whatever lay nearest in the laden cart, and ran away as fast as

153

my legs would carry me. It was the first time I stole, and no sense of shame stirred in me. I looked at the booty in my shaking hands. Three large pasties lay there. I stared and decided not to be in a hurry to eat them.

It happened in the neighborhood of the Tsarina Meadow. By that time I had forgotten all my earlier dreams about the Hetman, but the Summer Gardens lay beyond the Meadow and I thought it would be good to feast under the shade of those magnificent elms.

I tramped across the vast space of the Meadow, weariness gaining on me with every step. I plunged into the Gardens, made for a generously boughed tree, and sprawled under it. A wide avenue stretched to the right and the left, but the place seemed quite deserted at that early hour.

And then, my loot close to me, I fell asleep.

A stealthy movement somewhere behind woke me. I sat up and rubbed my eyes. Down the alley I saw two ragged boys running away as fast as they could. I looked to my left. The three golden-brown pasties were gone. The boys turned once, saw me still seated on the ground, laughed, and vanished around a bend.

Such despair swept over me that I could not move. Nothing mattered any more. It seemed the end to all adventure and ambition. Then I saw a tall man approach and halt within a few yards from me.

"So they stole your breakfast from you, the scoundrels."

All mazed though I was, I recognized my countryman in the man, but even that did not excite me. I answered huskily: "Well, yes, but I stole it first."

He came nearer still and sprawled on the ground beside me. He wore no wig and his brown hair was unkempt, his green coat and breeches were shabby and stained, his linen none too fresh, his shoes dusty. A faint breath of compassion stirred in me. Had he, like me, tramped all the long, long way to the north to find his fortune, and failed?

Without a word the man pushed his hand into his pocket and pulled out a couple of wheaten rusks, an apple, and an onion.

"Eat," he said tersely, and turned his face away.

I wolfed it all down. I did not even remember to thank him. With the last crumb gone, I stammered, "But wasn't it your breakfast? You are my countryman. I am sorry—you and I seem to be in the same boat."

He still kept his face away. He said quite casually in Ukrainian, "Well, I was not as hungry as you. What brought you here?"

"My voice," I mumbled, the admission surprising myself.

He turned toward me. His eyes were dark blue and very big. As I looked, I said to myself that I had never met so handsome a man.

"Tell me."

I did, from the very beginning, stumbling and faltering. It must have seemed a most muddled chronicle—I was in no condition to bring out a consecutive narrative. The shabby stranger never interrupted. He listened, idly chewing one blade of grass after another. So I came to the end.

"See, there was nobody I wanted to meet in St. Petersburg except the Hetman, and now that I have heard all these things about him, well—" I shrugged. "Market women may gossip, I know, but those two elegant people in the barge—they must have known."

"Yes," he agreed rather sadly. "I, too, have heard about

those things. You see, lad, jealousy is a worse thing than murder, to my mind."

I did not quite understand what he meant, and I said so, but he did not explain.

"And what were you thinking of doing? Just starve here?"

I hung my head.

"Would you like to come with me?"

"Are you going back to Ukraina, then?"

"Do you want to go back?"

I shook my head.

"N-no. If I could only prove it to myself that the Hetman has no heart. But how can I do it? His door was slammed in my face when I was decently clad—and now—" and again I hung my head.

"Slammed in your face, lad? Well, that is not likely to happen again," and before I could draw a breath, he added very quietly, "I am the Hetman."

13

"It Must Be a Dream!"

You know what often happens in a dream—a detail flashes
clear, all but dazzling you, then it melts away, and another
sweeps in and yet another, all clear and swift and teasing, and
then you wake up, happy but confused, and you can't remember any separate detail but you know you have had a pleasant
dream.

So it happened to me that June morning in 1744, except
that I did not wake up to find the dreamed-of splendors
vanished from the horizon.

I remember sitting on the edge of a green velvet chair and
staring at a pretty gold clock enameled in red and blue. I
remember that I wore clean clothes which were not mine. But
I cannot recollect the moment when I must have passed
through that great door between two high marble pillars. I
cannot remember the room I was taken to, or the servant
bringing those clothes. I must have had a meal because,
sitting on that chair, I did not feel hungry.

But I do remember clearly the Hetman coming in, and my
face burned with shame when I saw him still in those old
clothes. I did not then know that it was a habit of his to take
early morning walks wearing none but the shabbiest, least-

cared-for garments. My shame came from the recollection of what I had said in the Summer Gardens. "I'll never believe any rumor again," I said to myself, remembered my manners, stood up, bowed, and waited.

"Well," said the Hetman, towering over me, "I must get ready for my barber, and a visitor is coming to see you, young man." He stopped, but I stood there tongue-tied, and he went on: "You said that singing has meant everything to you. What did you mean by that?"

I stammered, "Why, Hetman, it answered—"

"Answered what?"

I was still too mazed to speak coherently. "I mean—you are given something—to use—to please—and not just yourself. It is like a straight road to tread—not wandering right or left—"

I thought what I said was very stupid, but I could do no better.

"I see," said the Hetman, and left the room.

I crept back to the green velvet chair and sat down. It was a big and lofty room with pictures painted on the walls and the ceiling. I remember a large pink porcelain stove with silver stars all over it, chests and coffers of such incredible workmanship that I felt I must rub my eyes and look again and again. In front of me was a piece of furniture made of some pale wood. It had something like a ledge halfway up, and the ledge was made of cunningly shaped pieces, about the thickness of my forefinger. Some were white and some black. It looked so curious that I stared at it for quite a time. I could not imagine its use. It seemed far too narrow for a table and not deep enough for a chest.

I sat quite still until the door was flung open and the

Hetman came in. I barely recognized him, so splendid were his clothes—all garnet velvet with falls of silver lace at throat and cuffs; so handsome was his wig. He was followed by a small elderly man in black, whose cheeks were pink and whose eyes very clear blue. He had the air of a kindly grandfather, but for some reason I felt afraid of him.

The Hetman strode across the room and slapped me on the shoulder.

"Here is the lad who has tramped all the way from Ukraina because he knows he can sing." He turned to the man in black. "Please put him through his paces."

The gentleman bowed and went to that curious piece of furniture, saying to me, "Turn your back."

I did. The next moment a lovely sound broke in the room, its echoes dying slowly. Then I guessed. It must have been the clavier—I had heard of it and had never seen one before.

"Turn around," said the gentleman. "What note was it?"

I blushed a wild crimson.

"Don't you know notes?"

"No, sir."

"Nobody has ever taught you?"

Defeated, I muttered an all but inaudible, "No, sir."

He got up from his chair and looked at the Hetman.

"Have you heard him sing, Hetman?"

"My good man, when I came on him in the Summer Gardens a couple of hours ago, he was all but dying of hunger. What song could I ask of him? He has had a good meal since then."

"In that case, Hetman, perhaps you will ask him to sing now."

159

"Come on, lad," said the Hetman and leaned back in his chair. The elderly gentleman remained standing, his blue eyes staring at the nearest window.

Then I almost wished I had never met the Hetman. I was terribly frightened of the man in black whose eyes seemed so kindly and whose voice and manner were frozen. And what song could I sing in that room, its splendors too dazzling, its furniture so unfamiliar? They were waiting, and I stood there like a block of wood. Then my eyes took to roaming right and left, and in a corner I saw a very ordinary, rather rusty cossack sword. It neighbored two or three magnificently bejeweled icons of Our Lady. It took me an instant to breathe a prayer to her. Then I began:

> May my sword be never stainéd
> By a shameful thrust;
> May my oath be never broken—
> Death to foe, life for a friend.
> Christ, my Leader in the battle,
> This I pray of Thee;
> Holy Michael, the Archangel,
> Of thy valor give to me—
> That I fail not, that I struggle
> For the honor of our faith.

I finished, cold sweat beading my temples. I saw the Hetman get up and make for a window, and the man followed him. The room was so vast I could hardly hear what they said, and I did not much care. I knew I had sung the cossack prayer for a newly found friend, and that seemed enough.

The elderly gentleman turned and looked at me. He neither praised nor criticized me. He merely said, "We are going to see much of each other." Here he bowed to the Hetman and slid rather than walked out of the room.

I stood rooted. I wanted so desperately to tell the Hetman that I looked upon him as a friend, but I did not dare. I expected him to say something but he kept silent and stood by the window, his back turned on me. After an intolerable pause, he turned and measured me with a strange glance. He spoke in Ukrainian, which might have made a warmth between us, but it did not because of the words he used: "Ever had anyone falling for you, Mark? You are very handsome, you know."

Scarlet to the lobes of my ears, I shook my head. He smiled as though he did not quite believe me.

"Ah well," he said at last. "But never mind . . . and it is time I went. You are to stay in my house and my servants will look after you."

I saw the door close. My face was burning, but I felt chilled to the bone, and I was confused, too. If only either of them had said one word of encouragement. Had I sung well or not? I could not tell. And what did the Hetman mean by telling me that I was to stay in his house? Until when? The splendor of the great room no longer dazzled me. I almost felt stifled by it. It seemed as though I were walking on quicksands.

Just at that moment the door opened and a bent-shouldered old woman slipped into the room. Under a neat white kerchief her seamed brown face looked so reassuring that I leaped to my feet and ran toward her.

"Come along, son," she said in a voice which had cream and honey in it. "I am Arina, the Hetman's old nurse. Oh,

Queen of Heaven, he has just left—all in tears, and he did not mind that the coachman and the postilion saw him cry."

I stared at her.

"What was the Hetman crying about?" I stammered.

Her faded blue eyes narrowed.

"It's all along of that piece you sang, son. The Hetman said your voice would have drawn tears out of a stone," and here she shook a bony brown hand at me. "Ah, but I must not say any more. You are to stay here till he is back, but I'll look after you, lad, don't you worry. Fancy you tramping all the long way here from Ukraina!" She caught her breath and went on, her voice wistful, "It is many a year since I was there last. I come from Kiev, lad. Are the cornflowers as lovely as they used to be on the fields by the Dnieper?"

For an answer I flung my arms around her neck. The rough, bony hand began stroking my hair. "Hush, lad, hush . . . I'll look after you, never you fear."

And I knew it was true. Old Arina was truly a twin sister to my dear Aunt Lusha in Moscow.

Yet I was not pampered in the Hetman's house. I slept in a tiny closet on a straw pallet. I had to go to the kitchens to fetch my meals, and the food, even if abundant, was of the plainest. I was given a broom to sweep my closet, and old Arina would set me various tasks in the garden. The clothes I had been given on my arrival were clean and neat but rather fustian in shape and color. All in all, not a member of that enormous household could have imagined that I was the Hetman's pet—which answered well since otherwise my position would have been intolerable. They had evidently been given orders about me—they kept rather studiedly aloof and I was not pestered with questions. To my relief, I never again saw the man with the triangular mole on his left cheek. Later, I would learn of his dismissal for pilfering.

Every day I said to myself, "I am in the Hetman's house because I can sing," and every day I wondered about the future, and sometimes I fretted so much that even the great garden could give me no peace. What was going to happen? The Hetman and the man in black had heard me sing—and not a word of comment had I heard on that occasion. It is true that I learned from old Arina that the Hetman had been pleased, but what would his being pleased lead to in the end? I did not dare put any such questions to the old nurse. Moreover, she had not much time to spare for me. The burden of the whole household lay upon her shoulders. From morning till nightfall she shuffled all over the house, giving orders, advising, scolding, and often enough finishing a half-done job.

I was assured of bed and board; I had reached my goal in meeting the Hetman, and I hoped I had a friend in him. I should have been happy. I was not. All the perils and privations of those long wanderings now seemed almost delectable by comparison with that splendid gilded cage, and often enough I wondered if I would ever sing again. I kept numb and dumb even when by myself in that great garden behind the house.

One week succeeded another. I cannot now remember how many of them had passed when one morning I found the mansion in a turmoil. Butlers and footmen were running in and out of state rooms, furniture was being rearranged and

163

polished, huge basketfuls of flowers carried in from the garden, new carpets laid down and old ones beaten and brushed, great quantities of china and plate taken into the banqueting hall, and all that to the accompaniment of incessant shouting and slamming of doors. Such an uproar reigned in the kitchens that nobody took the least notice of me and I felt sure that the platter of roast chicken and mushrooms a man thrust into my hands was a mistake. I did not see Arina until the evening, when she looked in, her wrinkled face rather solemn.

"The Hetman will be home by dinnertime tomorrow."

"Shall I see him?"

"God willing," she replied, and closed the door.

The very next afternoon the Hetman sent for me. He looked resplendent in sapphire velvet coat and white breeches, with a diamond star on his breast and jeweled buckles on his red-heeled shoes. His manner was so brusque that I wondered how I imagined him to be a friend. But he spoke in Ukrainian, and that lessened the distance between us.

"When I first saw you, you told me you had heard rumors —about my meanness and cruelty. Was there anything else?"

In a flash I remembered "the great secret" confided to me by Dolin. Was there any truth in it, and was the house being furbished up in honor of the Hetman's wedding day? Or was he married to the Tsarina already? At once I felt that it would be wiser to forget what I had heard.

"No, Hetman, there was nothing else."

His manner softened at once, and I guessed that my reply was the right one.

"I have a guest coming to supper tonight," he said. "I want you to sing at the end of the meal. You will be fetched when the time comes."

Ah, what a long afternoon it was, and the evening seemed even longer. At last it grew dark. I had long since eaten my supper, and I wondered if the Hetman had changed his mind when Arina and another woman came in, and I saw Arina put a finger to her lips. But the gesture was hardly necessary— such excitement gripped me that I was past asking questions.

Between them they combed and brushed my hair and dressed me in a clean white shirt and blue cloth breeches. I had never worn hose before and it was odd to feel them against my skin. The younger woman knelt to tie up the blue silk garters, and I felt as though I had become a changeling.

Here a knock came on the door and Arina called out: "Yes, the lad is ready, Tikhon."

An elderly footman in scarlet and green beckoned to me. Arina patted my shoulder and I tried to smile at her. Then I followed the man through one passage and another and across many big rooms brilliantly lit by chandeliers. At last we reached a great carven door. The footman opened it noise-lessly.

"Come," he whispered. "Stay here and wait."

The door behind was closed at once. I found myself facing a high, painted screen. In a corner stood a small table with two wax candles burning on it. From beyond the screen came voices and laughter, and the tinkle of glass against silver. I stood very still, my hands clenched hard.

Then the Hetman appeared from behind the screen and

whispered: "Presently you will hear a bell. Then you begin."

"Begin what, Hetman?" I whispered back, and saw his fine big mouth fold in a smile.

"Whatever lies closest to your heart," he replied and vanished.

I can't remember how long I remained there until the clear tinkle of a bell reached me. Then, as though by a miracle, all tension left me. I stood at ease, hands behind my back, head held high. "Whatever lies closest to your heart," the Hetman had said, and what lay closest to me was birds—all the birds I had known and listened to on the banks of the Dnieper: lark, thrush, blackbird, robin, nightingale. One of the very first songs I had learned stole into the memory, a delight and an anguish together. Then it broke from my lips. It was a short piece about a heron's flight.

I finished, and was half conscious of sweat beading my forehead.

There was such a stillness beyond the screen that I wondered if the room had been emptied while I was singing.

Then a woman's deep musical voice reached me: "Come forward, boy."

I moved. There must have been a crowd of servants in the hall but I saw none of them. I just saw a small table at the very end. I saw the Hetman seated, his head slightly bent. I saw a woman in violet and silver, the candlelight turning her eyes into sapphires. And I guessed who she was.

But halfway across I felt as though something were slipping down my left calf. I heard a smothered gasp somewhere behind me, but I went on. In the end I knelt by the Tsarina's chair, my left stocking all bunched around my ankle. She saw and laughed. Then, greatly daring, I raised my head and wondered why she should have tears in her eyes. I heard her murmur almost under her breath, "Oh, what a gift—" and I felt as though I had become kinsman to a heron on the wing.

Postscript

There was no more singing of songs after that—not for a long time. The Tsarina had me put to school, and I had to learn everything from the beginning, and my masters were far more patient than I. When my voice was trained, I joined the Imperial Chapels Choir. About 1750 I became Director of Imperial Chapels. With the years the Tsarina's benevolence grew and grew. She ennobled me, and was pleased when I chose a lyre for my crest. She settled two large estates on me, both in the neighborhood of St. Petersburg, approved of my marriage to a girl from one of the oldest princely families in Russia, and stood godmother to two of my elder sons.

My fortune has indeed been incredible, but the memory of my beginnings has never left me. With the Tsarina's blessing, I traveled to Bielogorka as soon as my training was finished, and made peace with my parents. On my way back I stayed in a little cottage close to St. Barbara's-on-Hens'-Legs in Moscow, and it was wonderful to meet dear Aunt Lusha again and to be able to ease her life by settling her in a proper shop in a better neighborhood. Later, I was able to trace Kolubin, and our renewed friendship lasted till his death some years ago. I also sent a letter to Abbot Iona, but there came no answer from Surazhy.

Now those who may read my story when I am gone might shake their heads and say, "What a lot he bothered about food through all his wanderings." Yes, I did so bother. People who are used to sitting down to regular meals every day might find it hard to understand what it means to go hungry and even to starve—and that not in the days of famine but in the heart of plenty. At Bielogorka I would take plenty for granted. During that long trek to the north I came to learn what it meant going without, and it was a good lesson. I beg all of you as yet unborn who may read my words not to dismiss me for a glutton.

I am writing these last lines in a big room of my mansion on the Nevsky Prospect in St. Petersburg. It has been good to remember that beginning. Now the candles are burning low, and I must go and open that little coffer in a corner. It contains my greatest treasure—a pair of very worn and certainly dirty bast sandals bought with one of my last coppers at Romny, I think.

I would like my very last words to be of gratitude to my Maker for everything in my life, joys and dangers, hardships and high fortune, and for all the friendships I have had—including that of the birds on the banks of the Dnieper.

MARK POLTORATZKY

On the Day of the Lord's Ascension,
 1779.

Explanatory Notes

THE ICON CORNER, usually known as the Red Corner (*Krassny Ugol*). The east corner of any room in the house, particularly the parlor, where all the family icons were hung. Underneath was a ledge for tiny candlesticks and a small glass oil lamp known as *lampada*. Candles would be lit on the vigil of any feast. Any guest coming into the house would pay homage to the Red Corner (usually by crossing himself and bowing) before greeting the host and hostess.

THE TRIPLE KISS. The customary Easter greeting was in three parts: "Christ is risen" (*Khristoss voskresse*), "He is risen indeed" (*Voisstinu voskresse*), and "Amen" (*Amin*). This was accompanied by three kisses—right cheek, left cheek, and right cheek again. Even strangers would exchange that greeting on coming out of church.

PECHERA ABBEY (*Kievo-Pecherskaya Lavra*). The oldest monastic foundation in Ukraina, dating back to the eleventh century. It was the home of the first Russian chronicler, Nestor. It was sometimes known as the Russian Mount Athos.

171

Its wealth was immense, since a great many reigning princes ended their days there—sometimes as laymen but more frequently as monks. Its repute stood very high. It was particularly famous for its hermitages—all of them caves in the rocks on the banks of the Dnieper.

LENTEN OBSERVANCE. There was the Great Lent (*Veliky Post*), i.e., the forty days before Easter, beginning on the Pure Monday following Carnival Sunday; and there were quite a number of lesser Lents—usually preceding some great festival. No animal food might then be eaten—cheese, butter, milk, and eggs coming into that category. Sugar was included because animal bones were used in the refining. Fish alone was permitted, since "by God's will nothing of animal nature could live under the water." It was rather odd that honey did not come under the ban.

OVER THE RAPIDS—a very old Ukrainian song.

IN MARK'S CHILDHOOD the Empress of Russia was one Anna (1730–40), niece of Peter the Great. Anna was a widow when she ascended the throne, and had no children. She summoned a favorite niece of hers, one Anne-Leopoldine, Princess of Mecklenburg-Schwerin, to St. Petersburg, had her married to Prince Anthony Ulrich of Brunswick, and when a son was born to them in July 1740, the Empress Anna proclaimed him heir and had him christened Ivan in memory of her father, Tsar Ivan V, Peter the Great's half brother. Anna died very suddenly in October 1740, and the baby Emperor's parents became regents. But the nation and particularly the army were discontented because "the Germans were in the ascendant everywhere." Little Ivan VI reigned for slightly more than a year. In December 1741, Peter the Great's only surviving daughter, Elizabeth, called on the guards' regiments to proclaim her Empress. Ivan VI was deposed, not a drop of blood having been shed either by his adherents or by the guards. Elizabeth had been engaged to a Prince of Holstein, but he died before the wedding, and she said she would never marry again. Her morganatic marriage to Count Razumovsky (called the Hetman, a Russian title of respect) was kept a state secret, and some later historians disputed its authenticity.

Glossary

ALTINNY   (noun, m., obsolete) A copper coin worth three kopecks, an old *kopeck* (*kopeyka*) being worth roughly one farthing.

BABA   A very tall, sweet, and lightly spiced cake eaten at Easter.

BOGODANNY PEREULOK   Literally, "God-given Lane," the adjective derived from *Bog* (God) and *danny*—from verb *davat,* to give. *Pereulok* is a composite word from *pere* (through, by) and *ulok,* derived from *ulitza,* or rather *ulichka,* "little street." Old Moscow teemed with such lanes running behind and between large streets. There used to be a God-given Lane in the city.

CHERNETZ   (noun, m., obsolete) Literally "a man in black." A popular name for monks, who always wore black habits.

CHERVONETZ   (noun, m., obsolete) A gold coin, its rough value about 30 or 35 shillings.

GALUSHKI   A favorite national dish in Ukraina. The nearest equivalent to it might be Italian ravioli—but *galushki* were not stuffed with meat. They were usually eaten with *tvorog*. Their meat counterpart was *pelmeny*.

GORNITZA   A word usually applied to the best room in a house.

KALACH   (noun, m., plural *kalachi*) A very light loaf made of wheaten flour and lavishly sprinkled with flour when baked. Of an unusual shape, something like a semicircular purse with a handle at the top. They were usually eaten hot, with a lot of butter. The best *kalachi* were made in Moscow.

KHOKHOL   (noun, m., plural *khokhli*) A contemptuous term used by the Russians. Literally it means a flock of hair falling down in the middle of the forehead. The Ukrainians were very proud of that flock, just as they were accustomed to grow their mustaches to such a length that—when at the table—they would tuck them behind their ears. Their chins were clean-shaven.

KHUTOR   Any steading, manor, sometimes a big farmhouse.

Glossary

KIBITKA   A roomy carriage with a hood, usually drawn by three and sometimes four horses.

KLOBUK   A very tall black hat worn by monks and nuns. The headgear worn by secular priests was not so tall and went by the name of *kamilavka*.

KOLDOON   (noun, m., f. *koldoonia*) A witchdoctor, a warlock.

KOROVAY   A big, flat circular loaf made of rye flour.

KOTOMKA   A satchel carried by pilgrims and beggars, usually made of sacking, some rough woolen material, and more rarely of leather.

KVASS   The favorite national drink of the past, slightly intoxicating, made either of rye bread or of berries. Raspberry *kvass* was particularly liked in Ukrani Ukraina.

MOSKAL   A contemptuous term used by Ukrainians and Poles in referring to the people of Moscow.

POPADIA   (noun, f., from *pop*. noun, m.) A priest's wife.

RUBLE   A silver coin worth one hundred kopecks.

RYDVAN   A very heavy and cumbersome coach which needed six and even eight horses to draw it.

SHAROVARY (always used in the plural) Very wide trousers, worn tucked into knee-high boots.

SVITKA A loose garment reaching down to the knees, sometimes worn against the skin, sometimes over a shirt. Either of linen or some light woolen material.

TABUN A collective word for any number of horses.

VATRUSHKA A large or small open tart filled either with jam or *tvorog*—a kind of rough milk cheese usually eaten sweetened.

ZAUTRENIA A very solemn Easter service which began at midnight and lasted some two hours.

ZHBAN (noun, m., obsolete) A jug made either of tin or of copper. In wealthy households it might be of silver and silver gilt.

ZNAKHAR (noun, m., obsolete, f. *znakharka*) Literally, "a knowing man," from *znat*—"to know." Practically every village had them. They healed (and sometimes cured) all manner of illness by herbs and spells. The clergy held them in suspicion because their magic was not always "white." Some among them were believed to be able not only to lay curses but to bring them home.